ALTERNATIVE

THE EDITED GENOME BOOK 2

MARCOS ANTONIO HERNANDEZ

CHAPTER ONE

TIME DEVOURS ALL THINGS.

The decay of a physical object is easy to identify. Time exacts its toll whether the object in question is alive or dead, evidenced by the presence of rust, the growth of mold, and the eventual return to the earth.

The decay of memories is subtle in the way it presents itself. There is no dust to be measured, no lack of color to be scrutinized. Instead, it is measured by what is missing. A lack of coherence, of completeness, creeps in over time until what remains is the skeleton of what was once alive.

Chloe surveyed the photo on her dresser of her grandfather and his dog and realized she had lost a small part of the memory from the last time she saw him. She could picture him in her mind as he picked an orange from the tree on his farm, she could hear his voice as he explained the way to tell whether the fruit was ripe, but she couldn't find the comfort the memory used to bring, couldn't feel his presence beside her anymore.

Was it because she had let people's minds occupy her body for money?

This question haunted her. Even if she had taken the time to recall the memory before she had been hijacked and compared it to the memory she now possessed, she wasn't sure she would have been able to tell any difference. By any measurement she could come up with, the memory was the same as it had always been, but the missing feeling, the diminished comfort it brought, made her wonder if she would lose even more of it if she captured someone else's mind inside her body.

Chloe knew she didn't have a choice if she hoped to invert the power structure.

She had returned to the city days before, after spending time on the island off the coast of the city. While there, she had been paid well to allow edited minds to take control of her unedited body. Chloe was the first human to have been uploaded into five times, an achievement bestowed upon her by the cordial enemy, WestCorp. The accomplishment was a source of conflicted pride.

Her friend Shada, also unedited, had had an even more historic experience on the island. While Chloe was relaxing between sessions of two-hour uploads, Shada had been trying to take back control of her body after she became the first person to accept a permanent upload. Michael Hollis, the leader of West-Corp, was dying and had made Shada an offer she couldn't refuse in order to allow his consciousness to live inside her body. Everyone assumed Shada would be lost forever, trapped inside her own body behind the mind of the edited man.

Shada had other plans.

It took time, and a few false starts, but Shada had been able to regain control of her own body, to everyone's surprise. What nobody had ever thought possible was that she would be able to access the mind of the leader of WestCorp, making his knowledge and memories her own.

Chloe had found all this out when she'd left the island with Shada. Neither of them was sure who in WestCorp knew about the theft of their leader's mind, but since they were allowed to leave the island, they both assumed there would be no repercussions.

Shada was back at home with her sister, in control of all of Hollis's assets. Hollis had assumed he would begin another life in her body, so he had transferred his vast wealth to her. Control of the company was another matter. While Hollis had control of Shada's body, and that body was still on the island, he still ran WestCorp, but everyone thought he was sick in bed and she was his mouthpiece. His terminal illness wasn't common knowledge, but his absolute control was never questioned, so the edited employees took orders from Shada without a second thought. Corroboration by the lead scientist, Alfie Reynolds-Grant, helped assuage any reluctance.

Now Chloe planned to go back into the power vacuum of the island, to capture a mind for herself. She wanted what Shada had, the resources and knowledge from a lifetime of work on the island. This was how she would invert the power structure, to bring herself and the unedited humans, or at least some of them, to a level above the edited.

She surveyed the dozens of plants that lined every surface in her studio apartment. In preparation, they were all watered, and the ones that needed sunlight the most were placed in front of the window, whose iron bars cast vertical shadows into the room. She debated making her bed but decided against it. She never made it anyways and didn't want to place extra importance on her trip. She had been in communication with Reynolds-Grant, who insisted she call him Alfie, and together they had made plans to replicate Shada's capture.

When WestCorp's lead scientist had contacted her, she didn't know if she should trust him. She knew Shada's opinion on the matter, that she should stay away from the island and be grateful for making it out alive, but the scientist said he needed to recreate his results. Since Chloe had been uploaded into before, she was the best candidate, and the fact she had talked to Shada and heard about how her friend had regained control of her body added to her qualifications.

Alfie had told her, "We both stand to gain from this," and he was right.

Chloe climbed over her unmade bed and reached an arm down through a small space between the mattress and the wall. There was enough space for her to withdraw a small safe. She entered in the code, her grandfather's birthday, and when the door unlocked, she withdrew two vials, one red and one blue. There were still four of each left in the safe, the last remains of a poison and antidote combination that took effect after eight hours. There had been many more vials, the last remnants of her mother's military research, but before each time she uploaded she took the poison then took the antidote when she returned to her body. She didn't trust the edited.

It had taken Shada days to first gain control of her body, so Chloe knew she wouldn't be able to take the poison before the consciousness was transplanted; she'd run out of time before she could take the antidote. She packed the vials with her as a kill switch. If she couldn't regain permanent control, she would find a window of time when she could take the poison and eliminate both herself and the edited mind inside her body.

Chloe put the two vials in separate pockets of her backpack so the edited mind inside her head, when it got there, would have no idea an antidote existed. Her plan seemed shaky, even to her, but knowing a kill switch existed made the prospect of losing her body to an edited mind more palatable.

She packed a change of clothes and zipped up her backpack. After turning to take one last look at her room, she decided to bring along the framed photo of her grandfather, throwing it in her backpack and closing the door on the plants. She promised them she would be back before they wilted.

CHAPTER TWO

THE COLORS of the city shed their typical washed-out gray hue and became more vibrant during Chloe's potential last walk to the train station. The bright wrappers of single cigars and broken balloons left behind from the night before seemed like the remnants left behind by beloved siblings. The smell of stale alcohol enveloped Chloe as she passed by an alley filled with broken bottles, an aroma she would rush by on normal days but one she savored now while walking at a steady pace. She shook her head at the mischievous antics of her neighbors.

She greeted the homeless men and women on staircases outside abandoned buildings and they scowled at her, no doubt wondering why she'd chosen this day of all days to acknowledge their existence.

This was a run-down, crime-infested part of the city by night, but the light of the day showed the shadows left behind by the darkness, shadows Chloe had never thought she'd miss.

The train ran on an elevated track. Below the track was a tent community composed of multicolored fabrics and structures made from various recycled materials. This was where the homeless children lived, their parents doing what they could to provide some semblance of roots. As far as Chloe knew, this was the largest concentration of homeless people in the city. She could afford to live in another part of the city now that she'd been paid for accepting the edited minds into her body, but she chose to stay in order to save money for her ultimate destination: a house outside the city, in nature, with orange trees, just like her grandfather's.

Chloe watched the children invent a game with a stick, a modified form of tag where whoever was "it" used the stick to extend their reach. One of the rules seemed to be that runners had to be hit on the legs, and when one boy broke this rule and hit a young girl on the back, the rest of the children surrounded him. They yelled at him, and were about to hit him, until one of them spotted a frog in a trash-filled puddle. The group of children all surrounded the amphibian, and the boy who broke the rules picked it up. Chloe climbed the rusted, grated metal steps up to the level of the train so she wouldn't have to witness whatever game the children came up with, not wanting to see the death of the frog.

The turnstile was stuck open, so Chloe walked into the train station without paying. A security guard, the lone person responsible for this station, was busy forcing passed-out individuals to wake up and either leave the station or get onto a train. None of the sleepers appreciated being woken up, but the guard, a no-nonsense older man, thin and wiry and sporting neck tattoos, wouldn't back down. In the end, some of the sleepers gathered themselves and left to lie back down on the other side of the turnstile, and some of them sat on the bench to wait for the next train to arrive.

Chloe leaned against a metal pillar and drank in the sight of the station she had been to so many times before but never appreciated. The billboard across the tracks, which would be hidden by the train whenever it arrived, displayed an advertisement for the current mayor, James Fitzgerald. The sign had been put up months before, during the beginning of his campaign, and now the bottom right corner was turned up, showing the bottom of the previous ad, a bright pink background for a product Chloe remembered as being marketed towards women. She couldn't remember what the product was. Graffiti artists had covered the mayor's face; some tags Chloe knew were local, and some she didn't recognize.

In the center of the platform was a large, broken analog clock. It had been broken for as long as she could remember. The time showed 3:41. She considered it lucky if she happened to be on the platform at the same time as what the clock displayed, and all but one time that it had happened had been during the day. Her nighttime witnessing of the correct time had occurred when she had missed the last train and slept on the platform, only to be woken up by the security guard in the morning. She'd stayed on the platform instead of walking home because the people who lived in this part of the city couldn't be trusted at night, and she was too inebriated to defend herself.

The train pulled up, empty. It had come from the depot at the end of the line. This was the farthest station from the center of the city, and with its reputation, one of the least used. Chloe boarded the train and took a seat beneath Mayor Fitzgerald's gaze. For the first time, she wondered why the candidate had chosen to waste his advertisement in this type of neighborhood. His smiling face was left behind as the train began to move.

While the train traveled into the heart of the city, stopping and starting with regularity to allow more people to board for their morning commutes, Chloe thought about what she would do after capturing the mind of the edited island-dweller. The first thing, of course, would be to go see Shada, to share the news with her friend. Not to throw it in her face, but to convince her it was possible for others to capture minds and, in the process, eliminate edited humans. Chloe wanted to turn the process Shada had discovered into an advantage for all the unedited. Plus, her friend would be able to provide insights about keeping a consciousness under control while it struggled to exert its will over a shared body. Since Shada was the person who'd developed the method, which revolved around learning to control the breath then listen to the heartbeat, it was important for Chloe to be aware of any of Shada's further insights.

Shada was a guru in Chloe's eyes, even though she shunned the responsibility.

Chloe got off the train at the center of the city. She descended two levels down to a platform nobody used unless they had specific business with WestCorp.

The difference between the public platform above and the private platform below was immediate and all-consuming. The public area above was decades old, and the accumulation of time and the passage of millions of passengers had rubbed smooth every surface and infused the space with dense, musty air. In contrast, WestCorp's private platform was bright, clean, and modern, with plenty of room to sit and attendants on the far side willing to help in whatever way possible. If WestCorp didn't have such a negative reputation in the city, more people would visit the space just to get away from the bustle above. But their reputation did exist, and couldn't be changed, so the few people present had more than enough space for themselves.

As Chloe waited for the tram that would take her to the island, she thought about how she wanted her house outside the city to have the same ambience as this space. The money she had made for the previous uploads ensured she had a comfortable life, but if she could pull off this heist, she could buy the house of her dreams and escape the rat race altogether.

CHAPTER THREE

CHLOE BOARDED the tram bound for the island, along with the morning's commuters. One older gentleman, dressed in a suit and tie and carrying himself in a way that made Chloe believe he was playing businessman for the day, stared at her as the tram began to move. She had gotten used to the sideways looks ever since she'd begun wearing numerous piercings in her ears, but people began to hold their gazes longer when she got her septum pierced. She smiled at the man, and he didn't return the gesture, instead pretending to look out the window behind her, as if he wanted to watch the walls of the tunnel pass by.

A display at the front of the car told passengers it would be eleven minutes before they got to the island. There weren't any other stops on their route, so it would be a straight shot. It also displayed the time—just after nine in the morning—and Chloe thought about the stark difference between the digital display on board the tram and the broken analog clock at the train station closest to her home.

The tram left the tunnel beneath the city and began a steady climb onto an elevated track above the bay. Chloe wondered how much energy was required to maintain the tram's speed as it ascended and how much was their momentum being used to carry them to the greater height. With the bay extending on both sides of her car, she could see far into the distance, until the clouds overhead met the water on the horizon. As the city receded, she visualized coming back with someone else's mind residing in her body. Failure wasn't an option.

The other passengers on board didn't share her relaxed demeanor. They either seemed to be on their way to conduct business, based on the way they were dressed, or seemed nervous, if they were dressed as if they'd come from the standard population of the city. Numerous pairs of searching eyes, not seeking to judge but seeking to connect, peered at other passengers. Chloe could tell these people were unedited and were headed to the island to become happier, healthier, and smarter.

Chloe felt a connection to the unedited on their way to the island, appreciating their bravery for crossing the chasm that separated the two types of people. She had been one of them, once, but it felt so long ago. On her trip to become edited herself, a procedure that would launch her into a career with WestCorp, she had met Shada. Shada had been more vocal about the apprehension they both shared, but each other's presence helped calm their nerves.

The tram came to a stop below the center of the island. When the doors opened, the people she assumed were there for business lined up at the doors, waiting for them to open, and the ones Chloe assumed were unedited stayed seated, as if to delay their arrival. The man she had caught staring at her face was the lone passenger who didn't follow this pattern. When he stayed seated, Chloe wondered if he'd dressed in a suit and tie not because he had important business with the company, but because the unedited part of him was here to die, and this was how he wanted to be dressed in the coffin.

Everyone filed out when the doors opened. Before anyone could go up the stairs, they had to be searched by the pair of massive humans posted on each side of the staircase. The travelers formed two lines on their own, each line waiting for one of the guards, and since each search was quick, both lines stayed moving. These guards, Chloe knew, were designed this way, made to be laborers for the company. They towered over everyone present and reminded Chloe of trolls from the fantasy stories she'd been read as a child. The searches seemed to be a formality, evidenced by the fact that the large humans continued their conversation the entire time, and Chloe assumed they were looking for something specific, like firearms. She had passed through the checkpoint with numerous vials of poison and antidote the last time she came to the island and the guards never found them, or if they did, never bothered to withdraw them from her backpack.

When it was Chloe's turn, she stepped forward and was dwarfed by the immense amount of flesh next to her. It could have been because they recognized her, or maybe they deemed her to be no threat to the members of the island, but a cursory pat down and quick peek into her backpack was all it took before she was waved through.

She climbed the wide staircase and found herself in the large, glass-covered atrium. This was the hub of the island, the central location where the edited humans could take transport vehicles to any corner of the island. Seen from above, the transportation system was a giant wheel, the paths of the vehicles the various spokes. This was also where the food court was located, the only place someone could purchase food on the island. Most WestCorp employees ate their meals here. As such a central part of the island, this space saw most of its inhabitants on any given day.

There were numerous restaurants offering a wide variety of food. Locations for coffee, pastries, seafood, and ethnic cuisine stood out to Chloe, all staffed by employees with white shirts and pasted smiles. She wondered if any of the food had been brought from the city or if it was all engineered by local scientists. If they could transplant consciousness, the creation of artificial food was well within their wheelhouse.

Chloe already knew where she had to go. The businessmen who were on the tram with her each searched the sea of faces for their contact, the unedited humans huddled together until a WestCorp employee gathered them together and took them in the direction of the lab, and Chloe went straight to one side of the space, to an elevator that would take her up to the head scientist's office.

She wasted no time walking, her long strides eating up the ground beneath her. She was eager to get the transplant over with so she could begin to take back control of her own body. In her head, she rehearsed the process Shada had described to her: find your senses, control your breath, and, with the help of a serum created by Alfie, listen to your heartbeat. By following the flow of her blood from the central station of her heart, she would be able to regain control of the furthest corners of her body.

CHAPTER FOUR

Alfie's office was locked when Chloe arrived. After a knock and a few moments of waiting, the door opened and the gray-haired scientist stood in front of her, smiling. He wasn't wearing his usual white lab coat; instead, he had on well-fitting jeans, a crisp white button-down, and brown wing tips, a look that distinguished him from other company employees Chloe had interacted with during her previous visits to the island. Their khaki pants, white polos, and stiff demeanor gave them a country-club, elitist sort of distance from the island's visitors.

"Come in," Alfie said, stepping back from the door and gesturing inside.

Chloe stepped into his office. Books with slips of paper between their sheets were scattered on every surface, on the bookshelf, the desk, even the floor. His white lab coat hung beneath a baseball cap on a rack in the corner. There was a steaming cup of coffee next to a half-eaten scone in front of his computer.

"Were you eating breakfast?" It was just after ten.

"Late start today. Ruby wanted to talk to me this morning.

She's in charge now that Michael is . . . incapacitated," Alfie explained. He walked around the desk and sat down.

Chloe knew the mind of Ruby's husband was in the city, occupying Shada's body. She didn't press the issue. "Did you want me to come back?" she asked.

"No, no, go ahead and take a seat. As long as you don't mind if I finish while we talk."

Chloe indicated that she didn't mind. She pulled the chair opposite his from beneath the desk and sat down, setting her backpack on the ground next to her.

He took a bite of scone then a sip of his coffee before typing on the computer. A few dozen keystrokes later, he returned his attention to Chloe. "Today's the day," he said.

"It is?"

"I thought we agreed on that. Did you want to push it back a day? It shouldn't be a problem."

"No, we can do it today, I just thought I might be set up with a place on the island before the procedure."

"Well, you won't need it once the mind is uploaded."

Chloe nodded. "Very true."

"Did you have any other questions?" Alfie asked.

Chloe racked her mind for anything she might need to know. When nothing came to mind, she shook her head.

Alfie's voice got serious. "You didn't take any . . . substances, did you?"

Chloe pretended to be baffled by the question, but they both knew what he was talking about. She'd assumed her pre-upload ritual had been a secret because he had never mentioned it before.

"I know about the poison. It takes hours to kick in, and you took it before all five uploads. I won't bother asking how you got it, we all have our secrets, but don't take it before this procedure.

You won't be able to take back control of your body in time to take the antidote."

"You knew?"

"From the first time. The system found it right away, but since the uploads were only going to last two hours, I didn't have a problem with you having your own insurance policy. But now I have to advise against it."

"Advise against or restrict?"

Alfie smiled then took another sip of coffee. "Restrict," he said over the rim of his cup. "I was trying to be diplomatic."

"I didn't take it," Chloe said with a half smile. "Since it took Shada a while to take back control. She told me how she did it. You'll be giving me the serum, right?"

Alfie was surprised at her request. "The serum? You want the serum?" Alfie leaned back in his chair. He steepled his hands for a moment before reaching forward for another bite of scone. He swallowed and asked, "The serum helped? Interesting. I wonder how?"

Chloe shrugged.

"I still have some left from when she was on the island, and it's easy to make." Alfie turned around and looked out the window behind him. "The serum helped . . ." he said, his voice trailing off.

"So who's going to upload?" Chloe asked, interrupting Alfie's reverie.

Alfie spun back around. He opened a drawer and withdrew a manila folder. Opening it, he began to read. "Ben Fisher. Seventy years old, retired. Former administrations specialist, still on call in case of emergencies." Alfie took a break from reading to add, "He worked closely with Michael Hollis." Continuing with the information in the file, he said, "Uploaded once before, enjoyed it. Minimal imagination and was content with predetermined activities."

"What kind of predetermined activities?"

"Sad movies, comfortable chairs, time alone to reflect. We make a safe place for them to cry. As an edited human, he never had access to these feelings, and in his old age he finds them fascinating."

Chloe nodded, and Alfie shut the folder.

"I've told him this would be an upgraded experience, longer and more intense. He has told the office not to contact him for the next two weeks, plenty of time for you to take back over."

"What's going to happen when he doesn't come back?"

"I'll tell them he went into the city and disappeared. I can make up a reason, maybe something like he was abducted by organ farmers. Nobody will care; there hasn't been a single need for him for years even though he's been on call the entire time."

Chloe felt sorry for the old man. She hoped he was never aware of how useless he had become. But she knew that even if it had crossed his mind, he didn't have the circuitry to be anything other than happy. The lack of emotion insulated him from the pointlessness of his existence.

Alfie finished his scone and drank down the remaining coffee, cooled by this point, in one large swig. "Shall we?" he said before he stood up. "I'll tell him to meet us there."

"Let's get it over with."

Alfie called Ben Fisher and told him to be at the lab at noon. He took Chloe back through the atrium, onto a transport vehicle, and into the lab. Once there, he navigated through a series of hallways until they were far from the entrance. "The uploading room," he announced.

There were two stainless steel tables inside, each equipped with a modified helmet, and a small machine on a table between them. When Alfie got word Fisher had entered the building, he instructed Chloe to lie down on the table farthest from the door and turned on the device. It emitted a low hum next to her head.

"We can't let you see him. His identity is supposed to be anonymous, and he is serious about his privacy."

Chloe laughed. "Doesn't matter to me. Guy's about to have the ride of his life."

Alfie smiled. "If this works, imagine what it could mean—" He shook his head. "Let's not get ahead of ourselves. Good luck."

"Don't forget the serum."

Alfie tapped his pocket and told her not to worry. He pulled the curtain between the two tables, blocking the rest of the room from Chloe's view.

The door to the room opened within minutes, and Chloe heard Alfie greet a man with a gruff voice. A slow shuffle of feet against the floor ended at the other table, and Chloe heard the old man lie down on the second table. There was movement on the other side of the curtain, and Chloe assumed the helmet was being placed on Fisher's head. They exchanged a few words, and the man confirmed that his office knew he would be away. Alfie poked his head onto Chloe's side of the curtain and asked Chloe if she was ready.

Chloe wanted to tell him to hurry the hell up but nodded instead.

Alfie double-checked with the other man as well, who said he was looking forward to it.

Chloe couldn't help but wonder if she could beat Shada's time to capture the mind.

Alfie withdrew to the far side of the room. The curtain bisected his body and he was able to see both patients. He counted down.

"Three . . . two . . . one . . ."

Alfie flipped the switch, and Chloe's whole world went black.

CHAPTER FIVE

CHLOE AWOKE to the familiar darkness around her. She had no sense of gravity, no concept of time, and the black of a vacuum was the entirety of her experience.

The first time she'd felt this sensation, during her first upload, she tried to panic, but without control of her body she never got past its initial stages. She was caught in a purgatory between states, the mind knowing what should be felt but without control of a body to follow through with the emotion. Each time the hijacks ended and she found herself back in control of her own body, she forgot how unpleasant the experience was. She considered herself lucky her short-term memory allowed her to forget; it made the following uploads easier to bear. There had been three more periods of being consumed by darkness—her first four hijacks—before her final upload and the first time she was able to find the light.

Chloe allowed herself to relax into the darkness, to accept it, and when her mind quieted down and withdrew from the brink of panic, she witnessed a small circle of light in the distance. It was so far, and so faint, that she couldn't focus on it or else it would disappear into the black, like a distant star. Instead, she had to look in its vicinity and allow it to grow large enough to hold its shape under her full attention.

Her first time finding the light had been while Ruby Hollis had control of her body. This woman had been chosen in order to get a response out of her former husband, Michael Hollis, whose mind was inside Shada. Something about being in Shada's presence had made Chloe aware of the light, and by the time she learned to relax enough to allow it to take over her awareness, she could hear Shada's voice. The light turned out to be her vision, but it was as if her mind had taken residence at her feet and had to wait to drift up and lodge itself between her eyes before she was able to witness the world around her.

Chloe waited for the light to take over her awareness, to see through her own eyes again while her body was under Ben Fisher's control. After she ignored it long enough, her mind began to rise, and she was able to watch the light's approach. She anticipated seeing the room the upload had occurred in, but by the time Alfie's voice reached her, she knew they were no longer there.

Once she could see through her own eyes again, she discovered Alfie was walking next to her through the lab's hallways.

Chloe felt paralyzed with sensory input from her eyes and ears but unable to control any part of her body. It was strange, because she knew she was moving around and could see the halls she passed through with Alfie, but none of it was due to her control. Like a dream, or a movie, she followed the action, trying to take Shada's next step: regain control of breathing. It took a number of scans before she found her diaphragm, but while the two men walked, she was able to sense it in the background and within minutes had learned to speed it up past her body's natural rhythm.

Alfie led Chloe's body, controlled by Fisher, through the atrium and onto a transport vehicle while Chloe practiced breathing. Not a single breath was taken by her body without her being aware of the air filling her lungs. The scientist kept asking how Ben felt, and with Chloe's voice he answered, "Fine!" every time, like a child being taken on a day trip to an amusement park.

Chloe believed he did feel fine. Anyone would feel fine if they'd had decades removed from their body. She wondered what would happen to the shell of the body Fisher used to occupy—if they would dispose of it or if they would keep it running in case of his return. She had to make sure the mind never returned, to prove to Shada it was possible for other unedited humans to capture edited minds.

The two of them got off the transport vehicle outside the dorm rooms Chloe had stayed in during her previous trips to the island. Alfie led Ben-in-Chloe to the same room she'd occupied during her last stay.

"Why can't I go back to my own room?" Ben asked, in Chloe's voice.

"Uploaded individuals aren't supposed to leave the predetermined experiences," Alfie said, as if his expertise was beyond reproach. "This is where you will get used to the body. There are other activities planned, but they don't begin until tomorrow."

Chloe took this to mean she had until tomorrow to take control back from the mind inside her body.

Alfie told Ben there was one more step necessary for an optimal upload experience. "A simple injection, it helps keep the body's original mind from fighting back against the upload."

Ben stuck out Chloe's arm, and Alfie administered the serum in the crook of her elbow. It took mere moments to act. Chloe felt control of her breath slipping away from her grasp. It wasn't long until she stopped being able to sense her breath at all.

Alfie told Ben he would be back with dinner in the evening and in the meantime to get used to being inside the unedited body. "Don't let your emotions get the best of you," Alfie warned.

"I won't," Ben-in-Chloe said. "I'm so curious about what you have planned!"

Chloe almost felt bad for the old man. He was so naive and had no idea their plan would leave his mind trapped inside her body for the rest of another lifetime.

Alfie smiled and left, shutting the door behind him.

Ben sat Chloe's body down on the bed, testing the mattress, before he got up and locked the door to their room. He went into the bathroom to inspect his mind's new residence in the mirror.

First, he leaned forward in front of the mirror and looked at the numerous piercings in her ears and nose. He gazed at her eyes, a light brown, and played with her hair.

Chloe searched for her breath and was frustrated when she couldn't find it. Every time it would show up in her awareness, she tried to use the same strategy, relax until it grew, but it never grew. It stayed on the periphery and wouldn't budge.

What did grow was her sense of connection with the world around her. Even inanimate objects seemed to emit a life force that called out to her and interrupted her attempts to focus on her breath. She felt a sense of wonder at her own reflection, an awareness of her own existence.

Ben stepped back and began to take off her clothes. Her body didn't respond to Ben's fascination with seeing her in just her bra and panties. Chloe sensed her heartbeat on the fringes of her awareness and focused on the sound, finding it easy to appreciate its resonance. It was then that she remembered the final step of Shada's plan, to feel her heartbeat and follow its flow to her limbs, and she chastised herself for forgetting. She gave herself a pass because she'd assumed she would still be able to control her breath, that finding her heartbeat would build on the previous step and not replace it.

Ben took off Chloe's undergarments, and he used her fingers to feel every inch of her most intimate areas. The resonation of Chloe's heart extended to every limb, and with little effort, Chloe was able to gain control of her hands to stop their exploration. Ben looked at Chloe's face in the mirror, confused. Chloe took control of her mouth to smile.

It took a few hours, with numerous false starts and attempts to regain control by Ben, but by the time Alfie returned with dinner, Chloe had mastered keeping Ben's consciousness from taking control of any part of her body, all while standing naked in front of the mirror. After hearing Alfie's knock, she bent over and picked up her clothes, putting them back on before answering the door.

"Hey, Alfie," Chloe said with a smirk. "I could've taken the poison after all."

CHAPTER SIX

Alfie couldn't believe Chloe had been able to take back control in just a few hours. He quizzed her about previous uploads, asked her questions about Shada, and even asked her to demonstrate physical tasks, like balancing on one foot, as proof.

Chloe answered each question without hesitation and was able to balance with minimal effort. "He's trying to take back control," she said after both feet were planted back on the ground. "It isn't hard to block him if I concentrate."

Alfie opened and closed his mouth, looking like a fish gasping for air while searching for words. In time, he managed to find the words he was looking for. "You're better at this than Shada."

Chloe blushed. "She told me how to do it. I wouldn't have any idea where to start if it wasn't for her. Hell, it took me until the fifth upload to get back my hearing and sight."

"Even after she took back control, she wasn't able to maintain it so well," Alfie said.

"I'd imagine keeping hold of a man like Hollis would be harder than keeping this guy in check," Chloe said. She walked over to the couch, sat down, and pulled the coffee table with the meal Alfie had brought on it closer to her. Dinner consisted of chicken, mashed potatoes, and green beans, a homestyle meal Chloe hadn't eaten in years. She hadn't seen a restaurant in the atrium serving this kind of food and wondered if there was somewhere else the edited on the island got their food.

"This was Ben's requested meal," Alfie said. "We took his order for meals before he uploaded, made it part of the experience. Looks like we won't need the rest of his orders."

Chloe nodded, her mouth full of food. "You want some?" she mumbled, gesturing with her fork to the meal in front of her.

"No thanks, I already ate."

Chloe devoured the meal. Alfie sat down and watched her eat.

"What's the plan?" Chloe asked when she finished.

Alfie shook his head and laughed. "Didn't think you would get here so soon. I guess tomorrow we will run some tests. I do want you to stay here for a few days and see if you can access Ben's mind, his memories and knowledge, in a continuous stream. Shada said she wasn't able to probe Hollis's thoughts without a direct inquiry, but I think it might be possible to have a constant awareness of his thoughts without too much difficulty."

"She said Hollis is with her all the time. I assumed his thoughts were in the background and she could listen in if she wanted, but maybe she meant she could always access his data if she knew what to look for."

"Like an encyclopedia she carries with her. That's what she told me. Over the next few days, I want you to find out if you can let Ben see and hear the world, listen to his thoughts, but still not allow him to control your body."

Chloe grew silent as she withdrew into herself. She tried to sense Ben's mind, but it felt out of reach, covered in darkness, like he hadn't yet figured out how to sense the light from the bottom of the well. She wanted to find out what he knew about Alfie, to remember previous interactions the two of them had had, but without anything to grasp, she was left with her own limited knowledge about the scientist.

"I can't even sense his mind at all. It's like he isn't even there." The effort of trying to sense Ben drained Chloe, and she felt a wave of exhaustion wash over her. Her eyes struggled to stay open.

"Well, he has to be somewhere." Alfie looked up, as if his thoughts were written on the ceiling. "Hollis had a stronger mind, I'm sure that had something to do with it. I hope Ben's mind isn't lost in there for good." He brought his gaze back down and looked at Chloe. "That's what you can work on the next few days, giving him space to exist without being able to take back any control."

Chloe nodded and confessed to Alfie she couldn't begin until tomorrow because she was about to fall asleep. Alfie told her the events of the day had taken a toll on her and to come find him whenever she woke up tomorrow.

"I'll probably be in my office," Alfie said as he walked out the door.

Chloe didn't bother taking off her clothes before climbing into bed. Her eyes gave up their fight, and a breath later, she was fast asleep. She felt anxious when she woke the next morning, as if the events of the previous day had coalesced while she was asleep and stayed behind instead of marching forward in time to meet her. She couldn't recall dreaming the night before, and she feared her own consciousness had descended into the darkness alongside Ben's, allowing room for him to take over her body while she slept. This thought terrified her, and she made a mental note to ask Alfie to monitor her while she slept. She hoped she wouldn't need to be tranquilized or restrained in the future.

She shook her head to clear her mind of these thoughts, stood staring at herself in the mirror, and reminded herself to stop catastrophizing before she left to find Alfie, wearing the same outfit as the day before.

Since she'd stayed in this building during her previous time on the island, she knew how to get back to the atrium. From there, she could try to find Alfie in his office, or if he wasn't there, she could take a vehicle to the lab. The day was clear, and from how high the sun was in the sky, she guessed it was late in the morning, though without seeing a clock she couldn't know for sure. Chloe looked out over the bay and wondered if her own mind was like the water, drifting out at low tide and allowing the island that was Ben's mind more space to maneuver.

The atrium was less busy than when she'd passed through the day before. She guessed everyone had eaten their breakfast and it wasn't quite time for lunch. From the clock over the transportation hub, she found out it was eleven, and some quick math revealed she had slept more than ten hours the night before.

As she walked along one side of the atrium, headed for the elevator, she saw Piper, the woman who had introduced her and Shada to uploading, walking towards her from the opposite direction. At a glance, Chloe was reminded why she didn't like the woman. It was her overall demeanor, the way she held her head and seemed to look down at everyone around her, both edited and unedited alike. She'd traded in her humanity for success in the company, and the result of her bargain was her proximity to Michael Hollis. In return, Hollis received her fierce loyalty.

Chloe wasn't sure Piper even remembered meeting her and hoped they would pass without acknowledgement. Piper's gaze was locked straight ahead when they were a few feet apart, unaware she was granting Chloe's wish.

Chloe's hand shot out and grabbed Piper's arm the moment they were next to each other. Chloe knew right away Ben had taken back control, and she cursed herself for getting lost in her own thoughts. The space her lack of focus created had allowed Ben to lie in wait and lash out at a time most advantageous to him.

"Michael Hollis is trapped inside Shada," Ben, in control of Chloe's body, said. "Took him into the city."

Piper stood dumbfounded, caught off guard by the statement. A flash of recognition, followed by rage, passed over her face as she looked at Chloe and her jaw dropped. "I knew it! I'm going to kill her."

Chloe knew Piper was protective of Hollis but had no idea why her first reaction was a death threat. She took control of her body back from Ben, let go of Piper's arm, and rushed away while Piper called after her.

"Hey! You, come back!" Piper called out, never using Chloe's name.

Whatever distance Shada had placed between herself and the island would soon be eaten up by Piper, who Chloe could tell wouldn't rest until Shada paid for capturing her leader.

CHAPTER SEVEN

CHLOE HAD no intention of going to Alfie's lab. First, she left the central building at the exit she needed to leave through if she was going to get a transport vehicle to the lab. There, she found one of the smaller pods waiting for its next passenger. She hopped in, said she wanted to go to the lab, and exited as it started to move. She wasn't sure if the vehicle would continue without its passenger and was grateful when it didn't slow down or stop. With her false trail laid, she jogged around the building in the midday sun and entered the central space from the opposite side. All told, she was outside for almost ten minutes, and by the time she went back inside, beads of sweat dotted her forehead. She looked at the spot where she'd encountered Piper; the intimidating WestCorp employee wasn't there. She searched the rest of the open space for the woman's face and was relieved to not find it. In a flash of inspiration, she popped back outside to see if the edited woman had followed her around the building and didn't see her there either.

The area around the entrance to the tram's platform beneath the atrium was occupied by a handful of people. Chloe wished there were more, so she could blend into a crowd, but her luck had already proven to be bad that day. She took a deep breath and walked with confidence towards the train station, hoping her efforts to ignore the people around her would result in everyone ignoring her.

She made it past the two massive guards and onto the platform without anyone looking at her twice. There was one other person waiting for the next tram, a forgettable man wearing an ill-fitting blue suit. Chloe guessed he had come for an early business meeting with someone on the island. His attempt at a stylish hairstyle looked like it was a remnant from his college days well over a decade ago, completing the look of someone trying to sell something inconsequential, like shower curtain rings. Chloe tried to search Fisher's memories to see if he somehow knew the man, but after his successful takeover of Chloe's body moments before, he had retreated back into the darkness.

She tried to give Fisher enough space to take back her right arm while she waited for the tram, but the edited man never took the bait. She knew she had to practice controlling the implanted mind, but how could she learn to stop his attempts at control if he never made them? She feared a repeat of what had happened with Piper, a coordinated all-out attack at a moment when she was lured into a false sense of security. In addition, she knew she would never be able to establish a consistent stream of his memories if she wasn't able to access them at all. It was like Fisher was engaged in guerrilla warfare, hiding in the recesses of her mind and waiting for the right time to strike.

When the tram came, Chloe remembered that the trip would be made without Alfie's serum. After Shada's insistence on the substance's importance, and her own experience being under its influence, Chloe knew she would have a tough time retaking control if Fisher took over while she was in the city. She wondered if the mind inside her had heard her and Alfie discuss the capture; if he hadn't, he might return to Alfie if he was able to take back control from Chloe. If that happened, Alfie could administer more serum and welcome Chloe back from the abyss. She didn't want to make plans for the worst-case scenario —if he didn't go back to Alfie at all—believing this might bring about its actualization.

The train pulled up and Chloe boarded. She was hit by a sobering thought: What if Fisher was able to hear her thoughts? If so, she would have to find a way to change her self-dialogue. Maybe she could follow her instincts without consciously considering them? Even if Fisher was able to sense the same bodily sensations, he wouldn't know which course of action Chloe would take, giving her a modicum of secrecy.

Chloe grew envious of Shada as the train carried her back to the city. It seemed more straightforward for Shada to be aware of the implanted mind, to know what it thought and experienced and sensed, instead of the open-ended questions associated with Chloe's silent passenger. All the while she wondered if Fisher, inside his own black box, was able to hear her concerns, or if they were both in separate black boxes, cut off from each other.

The train pulled into the hub below the city, and Chloe transferred onto one of the city's trains, into a seat much less comfortable than the one she'd occupied on her ride back from the island. The train had a layer of grime that made every surface appear sticky, with a stale, sweet smell to match. It was as if the train car had been left in the heat, and now that its services were required, the air-conditioning was turned on but no attempts were made to air it out. Chloe rode the train to Shada's stop, walked to Shada's apartment building at a speed just below a jog, and when the elevator took too long to descend, she ran up the stairs to the sixth level where the sisters' apartment was located.

A breathless Chloe knocked on the door and Sikya answered.

"Chloe?" she said.

"Where's Shada?" Chloe said as she stormed into the one-bedroom apartment. The room had minimal decorations and minimal furniture, one couch and a television, with nothing on the walls.

Shada walked out from the bedroom. The scars on her face, two thin vertical lines descending from each eye, were almost healed and were now thin pink slivers. They were the result of her loss of control to Hollis after the first time she had taken back control of her body, before she'd learned to use the serum to her advantage. Chloe rushed over, grabbed both her shoulders, and turned her around.

"Go pack a bag, we need to get out of here," Chloe said.

Shada wriggled free. It wasn't hard; she was much larger than Chloe. She turned around and looked at the fear in Chloe's eyes.

Chloe was struck by how weary Shada looked. It was as if her eyes alone had aged decades, the result of over a century of combined lived experience.

"What's going on?" Shada asked.

Chloe took a deep breath before relaying the events of the previous two days. When she finished, Shada looked at Chloe in awe.

"You've got a mind uploaded into you? And you took back control in less than a day?"

"Don't be impressed; he's stopped trying. That's why I wasn't ready when we ran into Piper! When I ran into Piper!"

Sikya, who had been listening the entire time, said, "I don't know why you guys think it's a good idea to mess around with these WestCorp people! I've devoted my life to helping the unedited, and the two of you get into bed with the people trying to keep us down! Now look what you've done: we've got some crazy woman saying she wants to kill Shada, and Chloe has no way of knowing when someone else's implanted mind will turn up and ruin things!"

Shada laughed at her sister before turning to Chloe. "She's got a point," she said with a turn of her head. Her expression turned serious. "I'm pretty sure Ruby knows I left with Hollis uploaded into my body. If they were going to come after me, wouldn't they have done it by now?"

"Ruby's in charge of WestCorp now. They think Hollis is in the bunker, sick. As long as he's out of the picture, she can be in charge, but if they find out Hollis is really dead, then the next person in line will take over."

"Piper," Shada said, chewing on the word. "Now that she knows Hollis still exists inside me, she could kill me, prove he's dead, then take over."

"That's why we need to pack a bag! I came here right after Fisher told Piper."

"And where do you suggest we go?" Shada asked.

Chloe shrugged.

"I know someone who can help," Sikya said, shaking her head. "I can't believe I'm getting caught up in this."

CHAPTER EIGHT

CHLOE, Shada, and Sikya took the train to the heart of the city, the more affluent business district and home of the Office of Unedited Rights. Their alertness never wavered during the entirety of their trip, looking out for WestCorp agents sent to eliminate Shada. The sisters sat edged forward on their seats with their backpacks still on their backs so they could make a hasty retreat if necessary, not trusting the other passengers.

Chloe was grateful the sisters appreciated the severity of the threat but couldn't help chuckle to herself about their lack of options in the cramped car. Where did they think they could go?

Sikya led the way from the train station to the office building. They walked past elevated gardens surrounded by smooth rock, and each open space in front of the buildings they passed had a fountain in the center surrounded by people milling about. Each of these people represented a potential threat, and Chloe scanned each face, searching for murderous intent. Sikya dealt with the threat by setting a blazing pace to their destination, walking so fast she could have been in a race.

Sikya led them into the light brown stone building. Before

the guard could stop them, Sikya told him they were "with her." The guard waved them through without a second thought.

Chloe was impressed at the level of familiarity Sikya displayed and realized she had underestimated Shada's sister. This feeling grew when Sikya went straight to the reception desk on the seventeenth floor and asked if Tensen was in.

"He is, should I tell him you're here?" the young Asian man said. Chloe recognized him from the last time she'd been here with Shada, when they'd set up the safety net for the initial hijacking of their bodies by WestCorp, but he didn't seem to know who the two of them were. It was clear he knew Sikya though.

"Is there anyone in there with him?" she asked.

"No . . ." the young man said, unsure or disliking the implication of her question.

"We'll just go in," Sikya said with finality.

She waved for Chloe and Shada to follow her. The receptionist stood up but never moved his feet, the index finger on his outstretched right hand attempting to create space for him to interject, but the three women ignored him.

Sikya pushed the standard wooden office door harder than necessary, and the three of them stormed into Tensen's office. The former candidate for mayor looked up from the papers on his desk and blinked, every other muscle in his body still. His phone rang, and he pushed the button to answer it on speakerphone.

"I'm sorry, sir, they just barged in."

Chloe heard the voice from two places at the same time, live from the room behind her and through the speaker in the office.

Tensen laughed. "It's OK, we both know she can't be stopped."

Hearing this, Sikya lost some of her edge. It was as if the acceptance of her disposition by the candidate whose campaign she'd poured herself into quelled her desire to cause a ruckus. Chloe could see why he was an effective politician.

Tensen ended the call, leaned forward in his chair, and rested his elbows on his desk. "What brings the three of you in today?" he asked.

Sikya cut right to the chase. "We believe someone at WestCorp wants to kill Shada and we need someplace to hide."

"From what I remember, the two of you went to the island for a procedure," Tensen said, addressing Chloe and Shada.

Sikya looked at her sister, confused that she'd been in this office before.

Chloe appreciated his discretion but thought it odd he withheld his information when Sikya had been so forthcoming with hers. She nodded, and so did Shada.

"And did everything turn out all right?" Tensen asked.

"For the most part," Chloe said. Shada stayed quiet.

"Then why would they want to kill you?" Tensen asked Shada.

"She took something that belongs to them," Chloe said, answering for her friend. "After their leader hijacked Shada's body, she retook control and left the island with his mind inside her."

"Hollis's mind is inside you right now? No wonder they're pissed." Tensen took a moment to digest. "But wouldn't killing you kill their leader too?"

"It's complicated," Chloe said in an attempt to stem the flow of information.

"He was dying anyways, and the plan was for him to transfer everything over to me and live a second life from inside my body. I had other plans." Shada showed a mischievous smile, and Chloe wondered if capturing the leader's mind had been her plan all along.

"That still doesn't explain why they want you dead. Wouldn't they want him back?"

"There was someone being groomed to take over when Hollis died. Right now, everyone assumes he's sick in bed, so his wife is running the company. I'd imagine the wife's trying to find a way to make her position permanent."

"And which one of them wants to kill you?" asked Tensen.

"Piper, the one who was supposed to take over when Hollis died," Chloe said.

Tensen nodded.

"Why doesn't she just tell everyone Hollis is already dead?" Sikya asked.

"Because he isn't. As long as he still exists in my body, it would be possible to upload his mind to yet another body, or back into his old one if it still exists. Hollis is the one who built the company into what it is, and everyone on the island knows it."

Chloe began thinking out loud. "And if that ever happened, Ruby could claim she was keeping the company safe until her husband returned. She has a way out no matter what."

"Piper needs Hollis gone for good before she can show her hand," Tensen said, summarizing the situation. "So we need to find somewhere for Shada to hide."

Sikya groaned. "That's what I told you in the first place!"

Tensen smiled at her with a warmth that begged forgiveness for his need to understand the entirety of the situation. "I'll help, but I have a request," he said.

"What is it?" Sikya asked.

"It's not from you. It's from her," he said, pointing to Shada.

Shada looked at Tensen with the gaze of an elder seeing the totality of the person in front of them. He grinned, appreciating the attention, in no way shy of being seen for who he was.

"You said Hollis transferred everything over to you?"

Shada nodded, and Chloe was struck by the thought that her friend had known what his request would be before they walked into the room.

"There's a lot of good we could do with those kinds of resources. Would you be willing to donate to help the unedited people of the city?"

"And by helping the unedited people, do you mean donate to your next campaign?"

Sikya looked at Shada with the bright eyes of a young, hopeful child. The prospect that her sister would become her life's work's most significant benefactor had to have crossed Sikya's mind before then, but based on her reaction, Chloe guessed the topic hadn't been discussed.

Tensen flashed his politician's smile. "Who better to help the unedited than me?"

Shada looked at Sikya, smiled, then turned back to Tensen. "Of course I'll donate. We can discuss after I stop having to worry about a crazy edited person coming to kill me."

Tensen slapped his desk and made a fist in celebration. "Give me one second," he said.

He picked up the phone, dialed, and told whoever was on the other line to be at the office in half an hour. "We need a locker," he said before hanging up.

CHAPTER NINE

When the stern-looking man dressed in black emerged from Tensen's office, he had been with the politician for all of ten minutes. On his way in, he had ignored the three women in the reception area, but now he walked up to them, his face relaxed and deferential, and introduced himself.

"My name is Richard Rees," he said before shaking each of their hands. He was tall enough to be imposing but not draw attention, handsome enough to disarm but not draw stares, and his smile was warm without flashing too many straight white teeth. In short, he was made to blend in.

The three women stood, introduced themselves in turn, and waited for instruction from Tensen, who had emerged from his office and stood in its doorway. "Richard here will take you to the safe house," he said.

Shada and Sikya grabbed their backpacks from the floor and slung them over their shoulders.

"The car is waiting in the parking garage," Richard explained, moving towards the door.

"I'll be in touch with you once you're settled in," Tensen said.

Richard led the way to the elevator, down to the parking garage, and into an idling black SUV. Chloe, Shada, and Sikya climbed into the back, and Richard got into the passenger seat. The driver had an olive complexion similar to Richard's, a shade hard to attribute to any particular heritage. They spent a silent hour in the car, and Chloe had to look through the front windshield to see where they were going because the rear windows were too dark to see through. She believed they were still inside the city's limits but in a more suburban area, where single-family houses were the norm. The SUV pulled into one of the gated driveways, waited a moment for the gate to swing open, and parked inside the garage of a nondescript ranch-style house.

"We're here," Richard announced.

Everyone, including the driver, climbed out of the car and walked inside.

"This house has constant surveillance," Richard said. He pulled open the cabinets and refrigerator to inspect their provisions. "There should be enough to last today," he said, gesturing to the driver, "but Tony here will be back either late tonight or tomorrow with groceries and anything else you need."

When Tony smiled, Chloe wondered how such a charming face had ended up hidden behind the steering wheel for whatever group the two men worked for. "Just let me know what you want," he said. His voice was soothing, like aloe on a burn. She got the sense he was the kind of person she'd want by her side if events took a turn for the worse.

Richard looked at Tony and gestured with his head back towards the garage. "He'll be back," Richard said.

The two men began to leave, and Chloe announced she was coming with them. "I need a ride back to the central station," she said.

Sikya was stunned. "Where are you going?" Sikya said, her apprehension palpable.

Shada wasn't fazed. "Back to WestCorp," she said.

Chloe explained. "I still need to get control of Fisher. Which means I need the serum from Alfie."

"What about Piper?" Sikya said.

"She can't be everywhere at once. Avoid her on your way to Alfie, and he should be able to take care of you," Shada said.

"You support her decision? She should stay here with us!" Sikya lamented.

"Without control of Fisher, she's still a threat. What if he takes control while she sleeps and tells Piper where we are?" Shada said to calm her sister.

"She could give us away on the island too," Sikya argued.

"But if she's on the island, she can use the serum to keep control. Without it here . . ." Shada trailed off, not wanting to speak the worst-case scenario into existence.

Chloe was hit by a wave of self-consciousness, and she inspected the two men dressed in matching black outfits. She wondered if they'd been too cavalier by talking about the details of their situation in front of people they'd just met.

"Your secret's safe with us," Richard said, all business, interpreting Chloe's look.

"Can you take me back?"

"Of course," Tony replied.

On the ride back downtown, Richard sat in the back seat with Chloe. "Tensen told me WestCorp wants Shada dead because she captured a mind important to them. Why aren't they hunting you if you've captured a mind too?"

Chloe was apprehensive, but something in the man's voice convinced her to trust him. "I'm not sure I've been gone long enough to warrant a hunt. Plus, the person I captured isn't important; it was more of a test to see if it was possible."

"To see if what was possible?"

"If another unedited person, besides Shada, was able to capture an edited mind," Chloe said.

"And you captured this Fisher guy?"

Chloe turned and stared at Richard, measuring the man. His continued questioning made her second-guess his intentions.

"Hey, we're on the same side here," Richard said. "I've devoted my life to equality for unedited people." He pulled out his wallet, withdrew a picture, and handed it to Chloe. It showed him in a park with two young children, one in each of his thick arms. "These two are mine. I don't want them to live as inferiors just because we couldn't afford to edit them."

Chloe marveled at the devotion to his family. When she exhaled, she realized she had been holding her breath. "Yes, I captured Fisher. But I wasn't able to keep control, that's how Piper found out Hollis is trapped inside Shada. I'm the reason all this happened." Her gaze fell, and she looked down at her shoes, embarrassed.

"Don't be so hard on yourself! You've done something incredible. And now you're willing to go back into the lion's den. It's commendable."

Chloe was grateful for Richard's kind words. "Thanks," she said, not feeling as brave as he made her sound.

"Do you think the procedure could be done again?" Richard asked.

"Like capture a second mind inside my body? If I could get control of this one, I don't see why not. I bet Shada could do it."

"No, could it be done again to another person?" He paused. "Do you think Alfie would agree to upload a mind into me?"

Chloe was shocked. "If it doesn't work, you'd leave your children without a father," she said.

"But I wouldn't be able to rest if I knew there was a chance to weaken WestCorp and I didn't try. They would understand."

"They're too young," Chloe argued. She returned his picture, and he put it back in his wallet.

"Not anymore." Richard's mood darkened. "This picture was taken years ago. Their mother took them and left, said she was tired of how much I worked. But if my work resulted in a mortal blow to the corporation responsible for them being second-class citizens, it would all be worth it."

Chloe shook her head. "I'm sure they'd prefer to have their father instead."

"It's too late for that," Richard lamented.

Tony honked the horn at a car that had cut him off. Chloe looked through the front window and realized they were close to the train station.

"Let me talk to the scientist and see if he wants to run another test," Chloe said.

"Perfect, let me know."

"How can I reach you?"

"Tensen and Tony both know how to get a hold of me."

Chloe nodded, unsure how she felt about sharing the internal process to taking back control. Shada was the one who'd created the framework, she should be the one to guide him. But Shada had objected to Chloe's attempt to capture an edited mind, and Chloe believed she wouldn't want to risk someone else. Then again, Chloe thought, maybe Shada had objected because she and Chloe were friends. Since she'd just met Richard, she might not care whether or not he attempted the procedure.

The conversation never resumed, and Chloe considered Richard's request. In the end, she decided she would be able to describe the steps necessary for Richard to take back control, provided Alfie agreed to perform the procedure. Hadn't she been able to regain control of her own body faster than Shada had?

Tony pulled the car to a stop and a car behind them honked. He turned on his hazards and rolled down his window before sticking an arm out, waving traffic around him. "We're here," he said.

Chloe took a deep breath before she got out of the car.

"Let me know," Richard said again before the door shut and the SUV pulled away.

CHAPTER TEN

CHLOE TRIED to appear casual as she looked around the crowded atrium in the center of WestCorp's island. It was past business hours, and the tables were packed with people eating dinner. She was one of a few people who had come to the island at this hour; in contrast, the island's platform had been filled with commuters heading back to the city for the night. They piled onto the train as soon as she got off. Her fellow travelers hadn't paid attention when she lingered on the steps, letting them all go ahead of her. They entered into the island's bustle without pause, leaving her alone to peek over the railing and scan the space for Piper.

It had been hours since Fisher had taken control of her mouth to spill Shada's secret, and Piper's reaction to the information still hadn't revealed itself. Inside her mind, she couldn't find any sign of Fisher, but she stayed vigilant so the captured consciousness wouldn't be able to reach out to anyone else.

Convinced the atrium was Piper-free, Chloe stood tall and climbed the final stair. She passed tables filled with WestCorp employees and thought she felt a spike of awareness from Fisher, but the sensation was so quick that she doubted its existence. She was hit by a wave of nausea at the thought of losing control once more and wanted to get to Alfie as soon as possible so she could get another dose of the serum. Part of her was grateful so many people were around, so she could blend in, but if she gave in to her desire, she'd begin running at full speed.

Chloe realized she was sweating when she got to the elevator that would take her up to the level of Alfie's office. The events of the day had fried her nerves, and this most recent rush of adrenaline pushed her over the edge. She felt exhausted and missed her bed, both the one on the island and the one in her apartment, and wished she could retreat to the comfort of sleep. She knew that without the serum this wasn't possible, in case Fisher was somehow able to retake control while she slept. She became aware of how little she'd eaten throughout the day. She didn't eat much on most days, but most days weren't filled with the level of nervousness and constant awareness she had dealt with since the morning, draining her energy.

Alfie wasn't in his office. The door was locked, and when she put her ear to the door, she heard nothing inside. She had no idea where he lived, and the other place he could be, the lab, would require her going back into the crowded food court, a daunting prospect.

She closed her eyes and felt for Fisher. She wanted to know if he was going to make an attempt at her body so she could deal with it while she was alone, but there was silence on his part. She took a deep breath and exhaled, aware of her diminished capability to find and focus on her heartbeat. She needed the serum.

When Chloe entered the food court, she stayed on the edges of the space, hoping to use the perimeter to avoid prying eyes. In reality, she knew there was just one person who cared if she was on the island, Piper, so the slinking around and worrying was unnecessary. In addition, the first time she'd run into Piper was on the edge of the atrium, in front of a restaurant, but keeping a low profile helped Chloe believe she was being proactive instead of just hoping for the best. She made it to the waiting transport vehicle outside and hopped in, hoping Alfie was in the lab. If not, she could be in for a long, sleepless night.

Special identification was required to get past the waiting area of the lab. She had seen Alfie raise the badge on his right hip to the small black box next to the frosted glass double doors, but she'd forgotten that the lab required permission to enter. She milled about in front of the doors, her desperation growing, while she wondered how she could contact someone inside to let her in and help her find Alfie. She looked up and saw a security camera. Without a second thought, she hopped up and down and waved her hands, hoping a guard would see her and investigate. Her hope was to convince them she had forgotten her pass and they would let her in.

She paced the room, trying to assume the air of a frustrated scientist kept away from her work, as the minutes crept by. The door opened just as she was about to give up.

"What are you doing?" Alfie asked with a laugh. "The guards said some crazy lady was out here and asked if you were one of mine."

Chloe felt a flush creep up her neck before anger at her body's natural response settled in. "Where were you?" she said, as if Alfie was the one who'd left the island, not her.

"I've been working, like always," Alfie said, tired. "You were supposed to come find me hours ago. No way you just woke up."

"I didn't just wake up." Chloe nodded towards the camera overhead. "Can we go talk inside?"

Alfie understood and tilted his head back, gesturing for Chloe to follow him. He led the way through an empty series of halls and offices until they were quite far from the entrance. Chloe knew she would have trouble finding her way out alone.

"In here," Alfie said, opening a door for Chloe.

The room was much larger than Chloe had anticipated based on the size of the door. There were three stainless steel tables, and stainless steel counters surrounded the perimeter. It had numerous machines she had never seen before, some made of exposed wires and gleaming metal, others made of dark gray plastic. There were multiple computer monitors hooked up to various machines, and in a fume hood was a full set of glassware and small ceramic containers. The walls were unfinished, and every corner of the room was illuminated by bright lights overhead.

"Is this where you work?"

"Most of the time. This is where I built the machine to transplant consciousness."

"You have an office and this whole room?" Chloe said in awe. She realized how important Alfie must be to the company if he was the sole user of both spaces, and she wondered how the loss of the lead scientist would affect their operations if anyone ever captured his mind.

"The office is for theoretical work. In here is where I bring my ideas to life."

"And you use this all by yourself?"

"I have a team who helps me here and there, but for the most part, yes, I'm in here alone."

Chloe walked around and looked at the various pieces of equipment, curious about what they all did.

"Where were you?" Alfie asked.

"I left the island."

Alfie smiled. "I know that. What did you do in the city?"

Chloe told Alfie about her run-in with Piper and how she went to warn Shada. She kept out the parts about visiting the Office of Unedited Rights and relocating Shada and Sikya to another part of the city, unsure of how much she could trust the scientist.

"I spoke with Piper earlier today, as a matter of fact," Alfie said, as if to continue their conversation.

Chloe felt her bottom jaw drop and rushed to close her mouth. "About what?" she said.

"She inquired about editing for increased physical strength."

"I knew it! She's getting ready to go after Shada!"

"Perhaps," Alfie said, his voice trailing off.

"What did you tell her?"

"I told her the truth: that it would be hard but not impossible."

"You can't do it!"

Alfie's face turned to stone. "I can. But I won't. It's easy enough to test new procedures on people from the city, but if I ever got caught testing on employees, I'd be removed from my position."

Chloe appreciated the euphemism for unedited and edited people and wondered if "removed from his position" meant killed. "Did she mention anything about me? About me capturing a mind?"

"She didn't say anything about you or Shada, just asked about the edit. She wouldn't share that information with me though; she has to know I'm involved, since Hollis is the one who was captured."

Chloe stayed silent, imagining the interaction between Piper and Alfie. "But do you think she suspects?"

"Maybe she thinks you and Shada had a falling-out? There are any number of reasons why you might have told her; I don't think she would just jump to the conclusion you captured an edited mind. It's only happened once before, ever, so I doubt it's a viable consideration for her."

"I can't lose control again. Do you have more serum? I haven't had any since last night."

"I was finishing another batch of the serum before the guards asked me if I knew who was outside the lab." Alfie walked over to a large stainless steel container that reminded Chloe of a refrigerator. From the third rack from the top, he pulled out an array of vials. "This should last us a while. Long enough for you to figure out how to read Fisher's memory."

"I don't know if it's possible; he stays far from my awareness," Chloe said, picking up and inspecting a vial.

Alfie took out a needle and syringe, filled them with the serum, and told Chloe to give him her arm. When she did, he injected her in the crook of her elbow. Within moments, she felt the associated flood of awareness of everything around her, in particular Alfie, since he was the sole living entity in the room. She found her own heartbeat and felt the flow of her pulse to each of her extremities. There wasn't any sign of Fisher.

CHAPTER ELEVEN

CHLOE WOKE up the next morning to sunlight spilling into her room through the window facing the bay. A sense of calm emanated from her and was aided by the sight of water outside. She watched the small waves rolling into the island, and instead of drawing the curtains closed and climbing back into bed, which was her initial plan, she left them open and started her day.

There was no way to measure whether her body had belonged to her the entirety of the previous night, but without a hint of anxiety, she was confident Fisher had stayed inside the dark corner of her mind he had decided to make his home. Nothing surfaced when she tried to remember her dreams from the night before, making her wonder if her mind had descended into the darkness and joined him.

She dressed and was about to leave when she was hit with a sense of déjà vu, like she was reliving the morning from the previous day when she'd run into Piper and put Shada in danger. Her stomach grumbled, its way of reminding her of its requirements. She didn't know where to get food without going to the atrium and wished she had a way to contact Alfie. If she was careful, could she make it to his office without being seen? She cursed the fact that all transport vehicles ran through the center. She could always walk, but that would attract unwanted attention at a time she needed to lie low.

She sat down on her bed to think and the mattress called out to her, begging her to climb back under her blankets. Her stomach urged a different agenda once more, wanting her to leave and find something to eat. In the end, her stomach won, so she prepared to go to the food court. No way was she going to be caught without a plan this time. She would rush in, get food from the restaurant closest to the door, and leave right away, minimizing the time she could run into Piper.

When Chloe opened her room's door, she found a tray with a covered plate on the floor in the hallway. She grew suspicious of her neighbors, wondering how whoever had left the tray there could trust the people around her. She wondered if the other rooms were empty. She and Shada had been given rooms straightaway, she had been assigned the same room when she came back to the island, and she never saw anyone else. She made a mental note to ask Alfie about it later.

Chloe brought the tray into her room and sat it on her bed. Under the cover was a bowl of thick oatmeal and a banana. "Standard," she said to the empty room around her. She decided whoever had brought the meal must have left it within the last hour, because the oatmeal was still lukewarm and dots of moisture dotted the inside of the cover. The bowl was empty in minutes, consumed in large, rapid spoonfuls. Chloe stood and stared out the window as she ate the banana, looking for signs of life outside. She wondered what kind of security WestCorp had put in place outside the island's borders. There was no way they trusted water, their natural border, to keep everyone out. She imagined a private coast guard, but since she had never once seen a boat near the island, she decided they couldn't exist. She guessed there were underwater sensors looking for trespassers, equipped with mines for protection. If she slept in her room for enough nights, would she be woken up by an explosion from the bay?

Her daydream ended with the last bite of her banana. She put the peel into her empty bowl and carried the tray with the intention of leaving it where she had found it. This was what people in movies did when they had room service, so she guessed it was standard practice on the island as well. She used her hip to hold the tray against the wall, threw the door open, and used her right foot to stop the door from closing. There was a piece of paper in the hallway where she'd first found the tray. She set the tray down beyond the paper—if there was anyone else in the rooms with her, they would just have to walk over it—and picked up the paper. On it were instructions from Alfie:

USE THE TRANSPORT VEHICLE OUTSIDE THIS EXIT, IT WILL BRING YOU TO ME - ARG

This was underlined by an arrow pointing to the right.

Chloe stuffed the note into her pocket, looked back in her room, decided she didn't need anything else, then made her way to the exit Alfie had indicated. Outside was an unpainted single-seat transporter. It looked like it was a private vehicle, not one of the company's. Chloe guessed it belonged to Alfie, maybe Hollis. The leader wouldn't have any use of it anymore, even if his body had been kept alive. Chloe climbed in, and the vehicle began to move. At first, it headed down the path leading to the atrium, and Chloe worried she had been tricked. Then, all of a sudden, the vehicle lurched with the sound of changing gears and left the path, cutting through the manicured grass lawns between buildings. The open windows of the vehicle were small, and even though there wasn't any material between her and the outside, it would have been hard for anyone to see her face if they happened to see her renegade vehicle break the mold of traditional island travel.

The trip ended in front of the small building with a slanted roof, a single door, and no windows that Chloe knew was Hollis's bunker. Shada had shown her the residence of West-Corp's former leader before they'd fled from the island. The front door led to a room with an elevator, and below the island was Hollis's bunker, with multiple rooms and plenty of privacy.

The front door opened, and Alfie strode out. He met Chloe just as she was climbing out of the transport vehicle and gestured for her to follow him.

"This was Hollis's personal residence," Alfie said. The way he said it left space at the end of his statement, a sort of vacuum for Chloe to fill with her disbelief the leader would live in such a small building.

"I know, Shada showed it to me before we left."

Alfie seemed surprised, then angry, and his emotional journey ended with him being disappointed. "So you already know this is just the room where we catch the elevator?" he asked as they walked through the front door, his surprise ruined.

Chloe nodded.

They rode down in silence. When they got to the underground cavern, Alfie led her to what Chloe knew was Hollis's study. At the end of the hallway was the dinner table, so large it had to have been built in the space, and on the far wall was the inky black stone that served as the far end of the residence.

Alfie injected Chloe with another dose of serum before the two of them got straight to business. He was seated behind Hollis's desk when Chloe told him about the member of Tensen's team who wanted to upload an edited mind. "I can upload a mind into Richard, but I can't be held responsible for the results," he said.

"He understands that, he just wants to be a part of the testing," Chloe said. She was standing, leaning against the wall next to the door.

"And he knows about the process to take back control of his own body?"

"Not yet, but I'll tell him."

Alfie nodded. His demeanor become more personal. "What do you think about it? Will he be able to take back control?"

"I think he's stubborn enough to try. Once I tell him how he should be able to do it."

"But both you and Shada had been able to plug back into reality while hijacked, before your permanent uploads. It took you multiple times to do it."

Chloe liked the way he described the process as plugging back in. "Richard could be just as good as Shada, for all we know."

"True, but I have the feeling you and Shada are exceptions to the rule. We've been doing uploads for over a year now, and the two of you are the only ones who were able to witness their world while hijacked."

Chloe paused for a moment. "But you'll still go through with it?"

"Definitely. I want to find out for myself if an unedited off the street can capture an edited mind. I just wanted you to appreciate the risk."

Chloe was reminded of the two children Richard used as motivation.

"Let's discuss the reason I wanted to talk down here, in private: I need to find out if Piper told Ruby about Shada capturing Hollis."

"You don't think she suspects?" Chloe thought about the discussion she, Shada, and Sikya had had with Tensen but kept it to herself, wanting to hear Alfie's version of how the situation might unfold.

"Suspecting and knowing are two very different things. If she knows for sure, there could be . . . repercussions for me, which also means future uploads won't happen. And I don't know how we could get you the serum. It's easy enough to produce, but why would WestCorp scientists bother?"

"We also need to know if Piper knows I've captured a mind myself," Chloe said, thinking out loud.

"If she confided Hollis's situation to Ruby, she might have also told her about you. Either way, we need to find out."

"How will we do that?"

"You're going to be Ruby's personal assistant."

CHAPTER TWELVE

ALFIE'S PLAN was simple enough. In order for Chloe to work for WestCorp at all, she would have to be edited.

"No way I'm going to edit anything now, I've got Fisher in here," Chloe said, tapping her head. She thought maybe she should have tapped her stomach, or her heart, instead.

Alfie shook his head. "You misunderstand me," he said. "We will forge the record."

Chloe flashed a wicked smile, appreciating the scientist's willingness to subvert the establishment.

"The one problem is the money," Alfie said.

"How so? You can't just put it into the system as paid?"

"The money has to come from somewhere. If you could access Fisher's memories, you could transfer his assets to yourself and pay for it, but since he's been uncooperative, that won't work."

"Can you access his account?"

"In theory, yes. But it'll look strange if he paid for you to get edited, since you two aren't supposed to know each other."

"We could say he took a liking to me after he uploaded and decided to become my sponsor."

Alfie's head turned sideways, and Chloe was struck with the realization she'd said "we," as if she would be explaining anything to anyone.

"Who would look into it?" Chloe asked.

"The people in accounting are hawks, they don't miss a thing. What it comes down to is whether I want to pay for it out of the lab's budget or take it from Fisher. I can't decide which would seem less suspicious."

Chloe paced the length of Hollis's study. She knew what she was about to say didn't make sense, but she couldn't think of another option. "I've got some money from the previous uploads," she said, thinking out loud. "But I don't want to use it."

"It won't be enough anyways," Alfie said.

"What if we tried another dose of serum? If it increased my awareness, I might be able to find Fisher then transfer his assets to me."

"I'd rather not. Too much could leave you unable to distinguish the difference between your inner and outer realities." After a moment's pause, he asked if she would be willing to go into debt for the procedure. "It would legitimize the process," he said.

Chloe didn't want to tell him no right away, but she knew she didn't want to go into debt. Her previous five uploads had given her a sizable windfall, which she knew was almost enough to buy her home away from the city. She didn't want to put her future at risk.

Alfie, witnessing her hesitation, told her that whenever she was able to control Fisher, she would be able to transfer all his assets to her. "It would be more than enough to pay off the debt and have quite a few more zeroes than you were able to make with the uploads."

"What if I never find him?" she said. It was a fear that had been rolling around in the back of her head, and as soon as she said it out loud, she realized the nervousness she would live with if that turned out to be the case.

"You think that's an option?" Alfie said. He looked at her with the tenderness of a father who wants his daughter to believe in herself. "I pegged you as the type who wouldn't give up."

Chloe's gaze dropped. She was ashamed her confidence had wavered. "You're right, it's only a matter of time until I figure him out."

"That's what I think too."

Chloe agreed to take on the debt so she could undergo the procedure, although since she wasn't going to receive any genetic edits, she was going into debt for nothing. They made plans to meet at the lab later, in the afternoon, which would give Alfie time to set up the trail of paperwork that would keep the accountants happy.

"Can I use the off-road transport vehicle again? I don't want to have to go through the center of the island," she said.

"Of course. It's voice-controlled, just say where you want to go and it will get you there."

Alfie said he had some things to do in the underground bunker and that he would see Chloe that afternoon. He gave her a sack of vials filled with serum and instructed her to dose herself every morning and night. She left without going into any of the rooms, though she was curious to see if anything in the residence had changed since the tour Shada had given her. Her best guess was that Alfie had taken over and made the space his own, but this was just a gut feeling and had no basis in anything she'd witnessed.

She spent the rest of the morning bored in her room, waiting for the time to leave and meet Alfie. Inside the bathroom, while staring at the mirror, Chloe tried to sense Fisher lingering deep inside her consciousness. Twice, she thought she sensed his awareness of her, but instead of trying to fight back, which Chloe hoped he would do, he shut down and went back into the dark. She slammed her fists onto the bathroom sink, ran her fingers through her hair, and wished there was something she could do to force his hand. She would have been satisfied even if she lost control of her body, but it was the anticipation that got beneath the top layer of skin and picked below the surface where she couldn't scratch.

Alfie was outside the lab when Chloe arrived. He waved at her vehicle as it approached, and Chloe was struck at the way he had developed into a quasi–father figure for her. He led her inside.

Chloe was anxious, as if she was waiting for a moment of pain. She imagined she would sign a paper and that would be the press of a button, signifying her acceptance of the debt. Instead, when they were alone, Alfie told her everything had already been done. "You now have a twenty-year employment contract, unless you pay off the remaining balance yourself."

The lack of buildup was appreciated.

"One thing to keep in mind: if you were edited, you would be happy with your situation on the island. If you paid off the debt, you would have to leave because it would be suspicious that you ever desired more than what the island could provide."

Chloe thought about the implications while Alfie continued.

"Of course, once you get control of Fisher and have the money to pay back the debt, you should leave the island anyways. I just want you to keep in mind how WestCorp views the situation."

"Believe me, I don't intend to stay," Chloe said.

Alfie led Chloe to a large white cylinder with windows made of thick clear plastic. It was bisected by a cushion with a pillow on one side for a person's head. There was enough space inside to accommodate even the security guards, the most massive specimens of human Chloe had ever seen.

"This is what we use to edit DNA," Alfie explained.

"Much more involved than the helmets used for uploading," Chloe observed.

"Funny enough, the process is much simpler. It just requires more equipment. The upload is much trickier, but we only need access to the brain, so the helmet is the only thing people see."

"If I'm not getting edited, what are we doing here?"

"I still need to run the machine. I can duplicate the results of the procedure from another subject, but there's no way to get past the required surge of electricity." Alfie pulled a mechanical lever and the cylinder peeled open. He closed it right away, the cylinder still empty, then turned to Chloe.

"Ready to get edited?" he said with a smile.

Chloe nodded, and Alfie pushed the button.

The white cylinder creaked to life. It sounded like there was something spinning inside, and once it got going, a low whir filled the room. While the machine ran, Alfie explained their next steps.

"Ruby already knows you will be her personal assistant and is expecting you tomorrow."

"What happened to the one she has now?"

"Turns out she's the exact blood type we need for an experiment. Her assignment was changed, and she'll be reporting to the lab starting tomorrow."

"Ruby didn't care?"

"Everyone at WestCorp knows science is our main focus. The whole company was built on the backs of our experiments; if the lab needs something, or someone, then we get it. The best thing Hollis ever did was instill an appreciation for what science can do."

"What can you tell me about Ruby?" Chloe asked.

Alfie looked at the ceiling and his face turned thoughtful. "Nothing much. When you meet her, remember you're supposed to be edited. No more attachment to unedited people. In fact, you should learn to look down on everyone not on the island. And pretend to be happy all the time, of course."

"What if I see Piper while working for her?"

"It's not if, it's when," Alfie said. "Working for Ruby will give you a certain amount of protection. Piper wouldn't dare do anything if you work for the woman in charge."

"She could find out where I've been staying," Chloe countered.

"Nobody knows that but me," Alfie said with finality.

When the cylinder stopped buzzing, Alfie told Chloe to take the transport vehicle back to her room. "In the morning, tell it you want to be taken to Ruby. Her position is on the island's grid, and the vehicle can take you wherever she is."

"Wait, is everyone connected to the system? If I told the vehicle to take me to you, it would do it?"

Alfie laughed. "Yes, but why would you want to see me?"

CHAPTER THIRTEEN

CHLOE TOOK a deep breath and knocked on the door to Ruby's office. She donned a reserved smile, the one she had practiced in front of the mirror the night before, hoping to appear genuine without looking too happy.

"Come in," a high-pitched voice from inside the office replied.

The door opened without a sound, and Chloe strode in with feigned confidence. Slivers of bright yellow walls were visible between numerous hand-drawn pictures of birds. Their feathers were painted with watercolors, but it didn't help any of them appear lifelike. If there had been one or two, Chloe would have thought they were the work of a daughter or son, but the fact they were displayed with such prominence, and that there were so many, led Chloe to believe Ruby had drawn them herself.

Ruby noticed Chloe's inspection and sat up in her chair. "Do you like them?"

"They're a great addition," Chloe said. They weren't professional quality, but they served to hide the overwhelming yellow beneath.

"Just something I do in my free time," Ruby explained. She

gestured towards the chair in front of her. "Please take a seat," Ruby said. There was no indication that she recognized Chloe.

Chloe sat down, and Ruby began telling her the expectations associated with being her personal assistant. Ruby didn't mind if Chloe came to work after her in the morning but required her to stay until she left for the day. "In case anything needs to be done last minute," Ruby said as an explanation.

Chloe stared at Ruby's hair while the woman reviewed which correspondences needed to be sent to her and which Chloe could answer herself. It was an artificial gray, as if she had chosen a reasonable color to hide white beneath instead of pretending her hair was still the color of her youth. Her wrinkles were well hidden beneath layers of makeup, but the lines around her eyes appeared when she talked.

"Did you get all that?" Ruby asked.

Chloe rattled off the few names that Ruby required her to forward and mentioned that she would ask about any names not included on the list.

"Good," Ruby said with a smile, deepening the wrinkles at the corners of her eyes. The smile disappeared and she grew serious. "There's something I need you to do. Think of it as a sort of test."

Chloe appreciated Ruby's straightforward manner. "What's that?"

Ruby leaned back in her chair. "I understand you edited yesterday. Before that, you participated in a fair share of uploads."

Uncertainty made Chloe's nods slow and measured.

"One of those uploads was me. Did you know that?"

Chloe scrambled to act surprised. "I had no idea. Did you enjoy yourself?"

"Don't lie to me, girl," Ruby said. Her eyebrows narrowed,

bringing out the wrinkles in her forehead. "I know you and Shada were close. She must have told you."

Chloe doubled down and gave Ruby an icy stare. "She didn't mention you," she said.

Ruby seemed to doubt she wasn't important enough for Shada to discuss. "It doesn't matter, that's not what I want to discuss. The woman who organizes the uploads, Piper. Do you know her?"

Chloe felt her stomach drop, and her blood ran cold. She considered saying she didn't, but one lie was enough for the day. "I do."

"Good." Ruby leaned forward in her chair. "I need you to kill her." Ruby then stared at Chloe, measuring her reaction.

While Chloe concentrated on what she should say, she felt the stirrings of Fisher in the depths of her awareness and had to fight to keep her focus in the room.

"I don't know what to say. Can I ask why?"

"You can."

Chloe waited for Ruby to elaborate then realized she never did ask the question. "Why then?" she said.

Ruby smiled like a teacher whose student just realized the correct answer. "I don't trust her. Never have. I used to tell Michael all the time that she was manipulating him so she could take over the company, but he wouldn't listen. Now I fear she is trying to capitalize on his illness."

"Makes sense," Chloe said.

"Of course it does," Ruby snapped. "And for what it's worth, I don't trust you either. All of a sudden Alfie needs my old personal assistant and you come waltzing in to take her place? Sounds too convenient. This is how you can prove your loyalty."

"Do you have a suggestion how you want it done?"

Ruby thought for a moment. "No, I don't care how you do it. I'll leave that up to you to decide."

"What happens if someone finds out I did it?"

"Well, you'll just have to be careful! But even if you aren't, I should be able to tell whoever investigates to ignore you since you have no reason to want her dead."

Chloe held her laughter inside.

Ruby got up from her chair, walked around her desk, and motioned for Chloe to follow. She stopped at the desk outside her office door.

"This is where you will work. Like I said, it's OK if you get here after me because I often keep strange hours and get here early. But once you get here, make sure you let me know you've arrived."

With that, Ruby went back into her office and shut the door.

From then on, Chloe was at her desk by eight in the morning. Some days Ruby was there before she arrived, and some days the office door was still locked and Ruby would come into the office around lunch. One day Ruby didn't come to the office at all. On this day, she called Chloe and had her reorganize an entire cabinet of paper files behind Chloe's desk, all over five years old. Chloe sensed her boss didn't have anything pressing and was looking for work she could do, regardless of Ruby's insistence that the organization was a priority. When Ruby showed up the next day, she never looked at the files, either trusting Chloe had completed the work or not caring whether or not she did.

In between completing tasks for Ruby, Chloe tried to come up with how she would eliminate Piper. It wouldn't be hard for her to use her transport vehicle to find out where Piper lived, she thought. She could then show up in the middle of the night, but she doubted she was strong enough to kill the woman with her bare hands. It wasn't her style and would put herself in harm's way.

She considered using the poison she'd brought to the island with her, but she had no desire to get close enough to administer a dose and had no idea when or what Piper ate. The risk of poisoning the wrong food was high, and when the toxicology report was returned, Alfie would know right away who committed the murder. Chloe couldn't pinpoint why she cared if Alfie knew she killed Piper, but she knew she wanted to keep it a secret from as many people as possible. There was also a chance someone else would see the report, and she didn't want to force Alfie to cover for her.

Drowning was also out of the question. From what she'd seen, the edited never approached the water.

As her days passed at the desk outside Ruby's office, she continued to daydream about a solution to her problem. She tried to probe Fisher's memories but found them still beyond her reach. The more she considered her problem, the more she came to believe that the answer was dependent on her ability to reach into Fisher's mind. The two tasks became interwoven, the success of one dependent on the other. She never considered the reverse, that killing Piper would allow her to harness Fisher's mind.

CHAPTER FOURTEEN

WORKING for Ruby came with its fair share of perks. For one, Chloe was given access to the files of every employee in the company. She wasn't expected to do anything with the information, and her work never required her to access the data, but it came with her clearance. She had stumbled upon the information by accident one day while trying to kill time when Ruby was in a private meeting with a food vendor from the city looking to become one of the restaurants in the food court. Chloe was curious about the company Ruby was meeting with, Sunshine Foods, and searched her computer for information about it.

The operating system returned multiple results, from both the internet and local files. Chloe read about the company online first and found out it specialized in vegetarian smoothies and snacks. If it were to establish a location on the island, it would be the lone restaurant of its kind. There were two mentions in local files. The first was a calendar event, Ruby's meeting. The second was inside an employee's file, inside software Chloe had never used before. The file said that the man, Lane Onza, who was still under contract with WestCorp, was also employed at Sunshine Foods. Chloe couldn't imagine why WestCorp would want a presence in such a specific company not even in the technology sector.

Without a second thought, Chloe then used the software to search for an edited person of great interest to her, Ben Fisher. It turned out there wasn't much more to his tale than what Alfie had mentioned. He'd spent his entire career as an administration specialist, and after his utility had worn out, he spent his time playing online chess and poker. His file also included his income as well as his net worth. If she could ever access the funds Fisher possessed, Chloe could pay off her debt and afford to leave the city behind.

Ruby escorted her guest out while Chloe took a shot in the dark and tried to find the mind trapped inside her. She had no luck.

"Do you have a second?" Chloe said before Ruby walked back into her office.

"Sure," Ruby said with an artificial smile. "What's going on?"

Chloe wondered if she should lie about how she'd stumbled upon the employee's file but decided against it. "I did a quick search for Sunshine Foods and found out one of our employees also works there."

Ruby nodded. Then waited in silence. "That's a fact. Did you have a question, or did you stop me just to tell me something I already knew?"

"I assumed you knew," Chloe blurted out, not wanting Ruby to think her time was being wasted. "Why is he there? Were you using him to set up this opportunity?"

Ruby laughed and shook her head. Her hair stayed in place. "No, not at all. A lot of companies find our edited employees more useful than the unedited." Ruby said unedited with such disdain that Chloe felt her blood boil. "They can't afford a whole company staffed with edited, but one or two is rather common. If you were to look into the employees of most large companies in the city, you'd find they have at least one."

"I see," Chloe said. "I never realized our reach extended so far."

"You have no idea," Ruby said before walking back into her office.

Chloe wondered how deeply the edited had infiltrated into the city's society. Could they also be a part of the government? She wouldn't be surprised.

A short while later, Ruby popped her head out of her office. "Can you go grab lunch?"

Chloe felt her stomach drop and hoped she would be sent to a kitchen to grab a meal made just for Ruby.

"I've got a taste for a burger today. Go to the Cheeseburger Chalet and tell them I sent you, they know my order. Don't bother standing in line, and get whatever you want as well."

Ruby was back in her office before Chloe could agree or come up with an alternative that wouldn't put her into contact with the island's inhabitants. Chloe slid her chair back from under the desk, stood up, and began her march to the atrium, dread at the possibility of seeing Piper making each step laborious. Her small hope was that her time in public would be short, since she didn't have to stand in line; she could be in and out before they came into contact with each other.

Chloe scanned the sea of faces as soon as she walked into the island's atrium. There were dozens if not hundreds of people, filling every table, and more standing in line at every restaurant. No sign of Piper. She went to Ruby's restaurant of choice and walked right by the line of people waiting for their chance to order. If any of them had a problem with her jumping ahead of them, they didn't say anything. She assumed they knew she was there on orders from Ruby. She told the cashier that she wanted Ruby Hollis's typical order, and the young man turned around and told the cooks he needed "one of Ruby's."

"Anything else?" he said.

Chloe told him she wanted the same thing but with chicken instead of beef.

The cashier turned around and yelled, "And another but with chicken." He then instructed Chloe to stand off to the side with a small group waiting for their meal.

Every other order was typed into the computer at the front. The cooks in the back would reference the computer in order to determine what needed to be made. Chloe marveled at the efficiency of the employees, at their lack of wasted movements. They churned out orders, and the people who had been waiting for their food before Chloe dwindled until she was next.

The cashier waved her up and handed her a bag. "Tell Ruby to have a great day," the cashier said.

Chloe wondered if he was edited or if he'd commuted from the city. "Will do. Do I owe you anything?"

"No, you are good to go."

There was a moment's pause when Chloe debated whether she wanted to ask about why Ruby got this sort of treatment, but instead of opening her mouth, she turned around to leave. She then came face-to-face with Piper, and her mouth opened on its own.

"Chloe, right?" Piper said, pretending they hadn't met.

Chloe closed her lips and tilted her head to the side. She didn't want to believe the woman she was tasked with killing had just walked up to her.

"You're going back to Ruby's office, right? I'll walk with you."

Chloe felt Fisher's awareness perk up and closed her eyes, found her breath, then her pulse, and made sure she was ready if he made another attempt to reach out. She started back without consenting to Piper. She wondered if the cashier had told Piper she was there, if every person working at the restaurants had been told to alert Piper when Chloe showed up. At least Piper knew Chloe worked for Ruby; this would make sure the woman didn't try anything stupid.

Piper didn't say a word until they left the noise of the atrium. She waited until they were in the hallway between buildings to speak. The people passing them would receive mere snippets of their conversation.

"I understand you're close with Shada," Piper began.

Chloe kept her eyes forward. Her mind was torn between three conflicting goals: monitoring Fisher, protecting Shada, and completing Ruby's assignment. She knew she couldn't make any moves in broad daylight, but if she decided to, two of her problems would be solved.

"I know I spoke with the two of you, but I imagined your relationship with each other was due to convenience. But after you told me such intimate knowledge of Shada's . . . capture, I realized you have her confidence."

Piper waited for Chloe to speak and continued when she didn't.

"I don't know, nor do I care, why you told me. But I have a favor to ask."

"Why would I do you any favors?" Chloe said, the words dripping like poison off her tongue.

"Why not? I never did anything to you."

Chloe had a sudden realization. From Piper's point of view, the two of them had had minimal contact, and the information Chloe had divulged could be seen as a sort of olive branch. It didn't seem far-fetched that Piper believed them to be comrades.

"What do you want?" Chloe said, exasperated.

"I need you to help me locate Shada." Piper paused, then said, "She's in trouble, and I'm the only one who can help her."

Chloe didn't care about Piper's reasoning, but curiosity got the best of her. "How is she in trouble?"

"Ruby wants her dead. If she can kill her, and make sure Hollis is gone for good, she can take over the company."

Everything inside Chloe wanted to scream how Piper was the one who wanted Shada dead, that she had to protect Shada from her, but she kept her eyes forward and took one step at a time. Fisher knew he didn't have an opening.

An idea took hold, and Chloe stopped walking. Piper took two more steps before she stopped as well.

"What is it?" Piper asked.

"Would you like me to take you to her?"

Piper nodded, her expression grave.

"Tomorrow's Saturday. I had planned on relaxing on the island after a hard week of work, but I can take you to her instead."

"What time?" Piper asked.

"Meet me at the platform at nine in the morning."

CHAPTER FIFTEEN

CHLOE WAITED until Ruby was finished with her meal to tell her boss she'd talked with Piper.

"You talked with her?" Ruby said, amazed. She was seated behind her desk while Chloe gathered the trash from lunch.

"I turned around with our lunch and there she was." The burger's wrapper had some meat juice on it, and Chloe folded the paper and put it into the bag without a drop getting on the desk.

"You're supposed to take care of her, not talk to her. What did she say?"

"She wanted to know about Shada." After a moment, Chloe said, "For some reason."

Ruby stayed silent, a thoughtful look on her face.

"I'm not sure if you need me for anything on Saturdays, but I won't be on the island tomorrow."

"That's fine, I'll have no need of you," Ruby said. She was still lost in her thoughts.

"If Piper disappears from the island, will you make sure there's no investigation?"

Ruby's attention snapped back to the conversation. "You

plan on killing Piper in the city?" she said.

Chloe nodded.

"Good, we can pin it on the unedited scum."

Chloe felt her face flush red and kept her eyes down as she reached across the desk to gather an empty Styrofoam container. "That's what I was thinking," Chloe forced herself to say.

Ruby waved Chloe away. "I don't want to know any more details. Make sure it gets done."

Friday afternoon dragged by. Chloe was assigned few tasks, and the ones she did receive were done right away, each taking a few minutes of the slow-moving hours. Ruby decided to stay in the office later than usual and didn't leave until after six, which meant Chloe also didn't get to leave until after six. Ruby told Chloe on her way out that if she wanted food that evening, she could tell the workers it was for her.

"Don't do this unless I give you permission. Tonight I won't be eating dinner, so you can take the free meal in my place."

Chloe thanked Ruby and watched her boss walk out with the air of someone in a rush to take care of an urgent matter. She organized her desk and turned off the computer before she left. She decided against taking the free meal because she didn't want to deal with the crowd. Her personal transport vehicle took her back to her room.

In preparation for the next day, Chloe spent Friday night staring at her reflection in the mirror, trying to find and control Fisher. Her evening dose of serum coursed through her veins, allowing her to be aware of her heartbeat and follow it to the furthest corners of her body. She searched for Fisher for hours, wondering what it would take to find him and gain access to his memories. By the time she left the bathroom, the sun had left the sky, leaving darkness behind in her room's window. She glimpsed her reflection in the window and imagined Fisher's entire experience was something similar, looking into the darkness and seeing his reflection. If he hadn't figured out how to see or hear the world through Chloe's eyes and ears, how could he ever show up? Chloe lay down and fell asleep wondering how she could allow Fisher to see the world.

The next morning, Chloe got to the platform below the atrium fifteen minutes before nine. She took a seat on a cement bench to wait. A tram, filled with people in fewer cars than during the week, pulled to a stop, and Chloe watched the passengers disembark. She wondered how the number of cars in the tram was decided and if there was ever a situation when there wasn't enough room to fit everyone wishing to make the trip. The tram pulled away, into the belly of the island, and a digital display flashed that it would return fifteen minutes past nine.

Piper showed up right at nine, and Chloe wondered if the woman had been waiting in the atrium above for the exact time of their meeting.

"Good morning," Piper said. The woman flashed a duplicitous smile.

Chloe squeezed her lips together before uttering, "Morning."

Piper sat down to wait next to Chloe.

"Does Shada know we're coming?" Piper said after a few minutes of silence went by.

"She does," Chloe lied. "She said she's grateful you're willing to risk your neck to tell her about Ruby."

Piper smiled, giving the impression she wanted to help. It was as if she'd forgotten her own threat against Shada and expected Chloe to do the same. Chloe made a mental note to look into the effect of edits on short-term memory.

The tram emerged from the direction of the center of the island. It had one less car than before. Nobody else but Chloe and Piper were headed into the city, so Chloe assumed the number of cars was dependent on how many people were expected to take the return trip. Were the passengers now waiting on the platform below the city, or was the number of cars a guess based on historic trends?

Chloe took a seat right inside the door. When Piper went to sit right next to her, a cold look from Chloe made her reconsider, and she sat in the seat across. They were silent during the trip.

Once the tram made it into the city, Piper followed Chloe's lead without a word. They went up to the main transportation hub and waited on the aged platform for the run-down train. Chloe took the train she had taken numerous times before, to the station at the end of the line, the one that she used to get to her now-abandoned apartment. They got onto the crowded train and were able to get two seats next to each other. At each stop Piper turned her head to Chloe, her body language questioning if it was their stop, and each time Chloe stayed still. Passengers got off each time, leaving fewer and fewer people on the train.

An announcement rang out over the train's speaker. "The next stop is the end of the line."

Piper turned her head to Chloe, and Chloe told her the next stop was their destination.

The empty train pulled away, leaving the travelers on the platform. Piper stared at the graffiti on the walls, the dilapidated billboard, and the trash on the ground. Chloe felt home.

Chloe told Piper to stay where she was. "I'll call Shada and make sure she's still there." She walked a few steps away and pretended to make the call. She saw Piper notice the broken clock and tilt her head sideways, since it claimed the time was after three. She withdrew her own phone to check the time and laughed to herself.

Chloe reapproached Piper and told her Shada had moved

locations. "We'll have to get back on the train," Chloe said.

If Piper was annoyed, she didn't show it.

A gust of wind blew through the station, causing the lighter pieces of trash to tumble past them and onto the tracks. A screech could be heard in the distance, getting louder with each passing moment, signaling the approach of the train. Chloe took the smallest step back as she turned to investigate the sound she knew so well.

The headlights of the train appeared, and Chloe felt her heart flutter for a moment before it settled into impassivity. She assured herself she was making a donation, that the world would be better for her actions.

The front of the train passed the first edges of the platform. Chloe took another small step back and noticed Piper was staring at the approaching train as well. Chloe made it a point to stare at the billboard across from them and furrow her brow, pretending to be confused. Piper followed her gaze and stared at the mayor's smiling face.

When the train was mere feet from where they stood, Chloe pushed Piper as hard as she could. She had intended for the train to run over Piper, but the timing caused the woman's body to be in midair when the train hit her. It wasn't moving fast enough to kill her right away, or so Chloe thought, but it couldn't slow down fast enough to avoid running over Piper when she fell onto the tracks.

A sickening crunch of bones rang out as the train screeched to a halt, and Chloe looked down and saw pieces of Piper in the small space between the platform and the train. She turned and ran before anyone could stop her. She stopped in front of the tent community below the station.

"There's meat on the tracks if anyone wants it," she said.

Hungry eyes of all ages peered at her. As she ran away from the station, numerous people ran towards free food.

CHAPTER SIXTEEN

CHLOE RAN for as long as her lungs allowed. She had covered most of the distance to the next station before she had to stop in the middle of a block of restaurants. It was still early in the day, so the restaurants were all closed; they would be opening up for lunch. Once Chloe's pace slowed, the looseness in her legs caused her to almost trip twice—both times catching herself before she fell—because her feet weren't lifted high enough to clear small bumps in the sidewalk. As she tried to catch her breath, she felt another consciousness viewing the world around her. It was an out-of-body experience, witnessing of a witness.

"That was messy," Chloe heard Fisher say.

A surge of panic coursed through Chloe. She stood stock-still and tried to regain control of her breath. The few people who were walking in the same direction went around her and shook their heads at her sudden stop.

"Don't worry, I'm not going to take over. Right now I'm just enjoying seeing the world again."

"How long have you been watching?" Chloe asked. She didn't say the words out loud, instead thinking the words of their conversation.

"I saw you push her. I sensed I could take over if I wanted, but I was stuck in darkness so long the light blinded me."

Chloe focused on her heartbeat. It wasn't hard to locate, since it was racing, but finding the beat and allowing it to resonate were two different things.

"It's nice to see the world again," Fisher said. Chloe looked around, inspired by Fisher to take in her surroundings. Trash from the night before was piled on the side of the street, filled with holes from where rats had tried to harvest leftover food. The restaurants were between one to three stories high, but much taller apartment complexes rose up behind them. The restaurant Chloe stood in front of, a hole in the wall serving pizza and wings, had numerous stickers stuck to the inside of its front window. Where there was a bare bit of glass, there was a layer of grease that prevented outsiders from seeing more than a blur of what was inside.

"How long has it been?" Fisher asked, regarding his time in the darkness.

"A while," Chloe answered, not trusting him. She started walking again.

When Fisher fell silent, Chloe assumed he was enjoying the sights of the city. They passed the remaining blocks before the next train station in silence, though Chloe kept a vigilant awareness of the mind inside her. A sign for the station pointed straight ahead, and Chloe found the municipal concrete building in the distance. She asked Fisher a question that had plagued her for days. "Why did you tell Piper?"

"I saw an opening to take back control, and I took it. I almost told her I was uploaded into you but knew that would be too much to explain. You have no idea how invested Piper is in Hollis."

"I know she was set to take over when he died."

"Then you know she wouldn't be able to let that information go without following up."

"Then you disappeared. Why?"

"I was waiting for the upload to be reversed. In the darkness, I started thinking through my situation and came to the conclusion I'm in here for the long haul. That's why Alfie had me take so long off work. Do you know if my body still exists?"

"No idea, Alfie never mentioned it."

"And that serum you have just leaves me jumbled. Whenever you looked for me, I just went further from the light. Then, when I felt your heart skip today, I saw a window of light in the darkness. I'd thought I lost my ability to come back, you know."

Chloe said, out loud, "Have you been in the city before?" Chloe searched Fisher's memory and knew the answer before he said it.

A mother and young son walking by saw her talk to the empty air around her. The mother wrapped a protective arm around her child and they rushed by.

"Never. I spent my whole life on the island. I find it fascinating."

Chloe probed Fisher's mind once more and witnessed a memory of him in school, staring up at a teacher inside a room full of attentive children. There must have been close to a hundred, and they looked to be of different ages, all sitting straight up with perfect posture, attentive and ready to learn.

She was still walking and almost stepped off the sidewalk into traffic. A loud honk pulled her from the memory.

"It's not polite to stare," Fisher said. He said the words as if he was disappointed in her.

"Alfie was bugging me about searching through your memories. I won't do it if it bothers you." Chloe couldn't believe she was considerate of the edited mind's feelings. But then again, he'd be in there for the rest of her life, and she might as well make peace.

"Don't dig into the personal stuff. I've got no problem with you looking up facts for reference."

"How can you tell?"

"Because I get thrown into the memory too. These aren't things I think about most of the time, so it's jarring, to say the least."

"That's fair," Chloe said. She couldn't think about the last time she'd immersed herself in a memory. If someone else made her do it, she wouldn't like it at all.

Chloe crossed the street during a break in traffic, turned left, then crossed once more and approached the entrance to the station. Without questioning Fisher, or seeing his past in her mind's eye, she knew he was curious about the city's train system and had never been this close to cars. Through her new lens, it was like she was seeing the city for the first time. Dilapidated buildings between those in use, chain-link fences with trash captured in their many corners. Each aspect of her surroundings, which she had taken for granted all her life, now became a question of whether or not Fisher had seen something similar in his past on the island. He hadn't.

Chloe couldn't shake the constant input of "No" to her standing question of "Have you seen this?" as she waited for the train, boarded, and took her seat.

Each person's face was searched, and some of them reminded Fisher of a person he knew, or had known, on the island. Fisher never said so outright, but there was a sense of the fact from a feeling deep inside. It was like Chloe knew without being told. Overwhelmed, she closed her eyes and found her breath, then her heartbeat, just to be sure she was still in control.

"Better?" Fisher said. He didn't have a chance at taking over any part of Chloe's body.

"Much," Chloe said out loud. All but one of the passengers ignored her. The one who looked at her was a young man who Chloe would have taken interest in if she wasn't stuck inside her mind. From his attention, it seemed he had deemed her worthy of his interest as well.

Chloe transferred trains at the hub instead of going back to the island. She had to wait on the platform for a long time for the next train on one of the city's slower lines. When it arrived, she climbed aboard and, after a few underground stops, emerged into the sunlight. The landscape changed into a perpetual suburban sprawl, each house looking like the next. The train passed vast lots filled with cars in various stages of decay, causing Fisher to comment on all the wasted assets. As much as Chloe wanted to leave the city, she preferred to stay in its urban area over becoming one of the masses in an overpriced home, dealing with small yards and terrible commutes. Either she was leaving it all behind or staying in the thick of things, no half-assed exit for her.

The last stop of the train was a full twenty minutes' ride past the previous stop. Chloe knew Shada's hideout was somewhere close but didn't remember where. She called her friend.

"Hello?"

"Sikya? It's me, Chloe. I need a ride to your place."

"I'll see if Tony can come get you, he's in the city now. Where are you?"

"At the station."

"Which station?"

"Sinbad Landings."

"That close! You're practically here. I'll come get you myself, there's a SUV here we can use in case of emergencies."

"This isn't an emergency," Chloe said.

"It'll take two seconds," Sikya replied before she hung up the phone.

"Sinbad Landings," Fisher said, as if committing the name to memory. "It's like all these people sailed away from the city in order to live on their own isolated island, together."

CHAPTER SEVENTEEN

"You should stay here," Sikya said when they were back in the safe house. "You don't need to keep playing with fire on that island."

"I can't stay," Chloe replied. "I just came to tell you, in person, that Piper is no longer a threat."

"What did you do?" Sikya asked.

"She killed her," Shada said from the kitchen table. Her eyes stayed closed while she took slow, measured breaths. It was clear she was listening to the sensations of her body, keeping Hollis from taking back control.

Chloe could sense Fisher's awe at seeing Shada for the first time. He wanted to communicate with Hollis but never tried to gain control of Chloe. It was a desire without an outlet. Chloe became aware of Sikya's stare boring into the side of her head, as if Sikya was in the presence of a monster.

"What?" Chloe snapped.

Sikya frowned. "Did you really kill her?"

"What choice did I have? She wanted to kill Shada."

"I know, but still . . ." Sikya looked at Chloe's hands.

"I didn't choke her," Chloe said. "I pushed her in front of a train."

Sikya's mouth opened. Chloe looked at Shada and saw the hints of a slow nod.

"It's done, no point in getting hung up on it," Shada said.

"Does that mean we can leave?" Sikya asked. She turned, opened a cabinet, and pulled out a glass. "Want some water?" she asked.

Chloe nodded, and Sikya grabbed a second glass before filling them up with water.

"No, we still don't know what Ruby's planning," Chloe said.

Sikya placed a glass in front of Chloe before downing half her glass in two large gulps.

"You should have never uploaded that mind into you," Sikya said when she pulled the glass away from her lips.

"Don't bring this up again," Shada said from across the room. She opened her eyes, stood up, and joined the women in standing, her lower back against the counter and arms crossed. "You better get used to it. There will be more."

Sikya looked at her sister in disbelief. "More! The two of you have caused enough trouble. Why would you want more?"

"I don't want more. She does," Shada said, using her chin to gesture towards Chloe. "She and Alfie."

It was Chloe's turn to be surprised, but she wiped the look away with a hardened determination. "It wouldn't hurt to have a few less edited in the world. If we can make an unedited smarter and better off financially, even better."

Fisher, hearing Chloe mention finances, knew Chloe would search his mind for the necessary codes and passwords to transfer all of his assets to her. He resigned himself to the fact and in that moment realized he'd been given a second life. Not one he controlled, but the chance to share in the future of another. As someone whose entire career had been spent in an administrative role, he felt at ease acting as support.

Sikya paced back and forth in the kitchen. Chloe and Shada let her go, waiting for the thoughts swirling in her head to coalesce. "They didn't choose to be the way they are," Sikya said, her voice soft.

"But it doesn't change the fact they're the ones holding all the power in the city."

"WestCorp holds the power. Holds power over them too. They're just not able to be upset by the imbalance."

"So we're putting them out of their misery!" Chloe said.

Sikya glared at her.

"Most of the people on the island were born that way, right?" Sikya said.

"I suppose, I don't know the numbers," Chloe replied.

"Let's assume," Sikya said. She glanced at Shada, and her sister raised her eyebrows in expectation.

"So their parents chose for them to be edited."

"They were probably edited too," Chloe said. She scanned Fisher's memory and found out he had been born edited to edited parents.

"And keep going down the line to the first edited humans. They didn't know what they were doing. They were using technology to try and improve the world, not ruin it."

"So we should feel bad for the edited?"

"No, I'm not saying we should feel bad, but rather understand that it isn't their fault. This goes back generations."

"Wait," Chloe said. "Aren't you super involved with the advancement of the unedited people of the city? Why are you arguing for the edited all of a sudden?"

"I want the unedited to be equal to the edited humans. That means elevating our status, not tearing them down from the inside, one quasi-murder at a time."

"He was dying anyways," Shada whispered.

Both Sikya and Chloe waited in silence for her to continue. They didn't have to wait long.

"He's the one who wanted to take over my body. He never imagined I'd be able to take it back. Hollis only has himself to blame." The volume of her voice never raised more than necessary for the other two women to hear, and her tone stayed consistent throughout her statement, as if she was relaying facts.

"I wasn't calling you a murderer," Sikya said to apologize.

"If anything, he wanted to quasi-murder her!" Chloe said. "They brought this on themselves."

"And what did your guy do? Did he convince you to upload as well? Did he even know what he was getting into?"

Chloe turned around, closed her eyes, and found her body's breathing to keep from losing her temper. When she turned around, she found Sikya's eyes. "He thought he was going on an extended upload. He just didn't know how extended it would be," she said with a small laugh.

Sikya cracked a thin smile, and the tension in the room evaporated. "All I'm saying is we shouldn't punish the child for the parent's decision."

Chloe brushed off Sikya's parting shot. "Too late, their time has run out."

Shada chuckled and changed the subject. "Did you hear about what's going on with the mayor?"

"No, I've been on the island the whole time. It's like living in a bubble," Chloe said.

"I know, that's why I'm asking if you've heard," Shada said.

Sikya shook her head. "Smart-ass."

Shada told Sikya to tell her.

"The mayor's resigned. There's going to be another election, and it looks like Tensen has a good chance of winning. He was a close second last time," Sikya said with pride.

"Resigned? What happened?"

Sikya told Chloe about the scandal that had rocked the mayor's office. It all came down to an assassination. A lawmaker had been on his way to propose a law to decriminalize drug use, turning it into a mental illness. "The politician was murdered by drug dealers."

Chloe took a second to digest the information. "Why would the drug dealers want him dead? If addiction isn't a crime, their business would skyrocket."

"Part of the plan was to provide state-sponsored rehab clinics. As more people got healthy, fewer would be looking to score."

"And how was this all linked back to the mayor?"

"It came out the drug dealers were sponsored by WestCorp. Apparently, WestCorp had a deal with the mayor to use incarcerated unedited to test their post-birth edits. With fewer people being locked up due to drugs, they would have fewer test subjects and the value of their government contract would go down."

"A lot of people didn't want this law to get passed," Chloe mused.

"When it all came out, the mayor didn't even put up a fight, he just resigned. I'm surprised nobody talked about it on the island."

"I told you, that place is a bubble. To be honest, I'm not sure they care who's in charge, they'll just bribe the next guy."

"Tensen's different. He's one of us."

"That's assuming he wins the election," Chloe said, skeptical.

"The mayor's entire party has been caught up in the scandal. There's money passing hands everywhere, kickbacks and contracts that shouldn't exist. Nobody else stands a chance."

"It's really just a formality," Shada added.

When Sikya was sure of a thing, Chloe found herself doubting. But when Shada knew a thing to be true, Chloe never gave the fact a second thought and accepted it as a fact.

"Didn't you donate to Tensen?" Chloe asked Shada.

Shada nodded. "He made sure I sent the money as soon as the mayor resigned."

"What's going to happen when someone finds out Hollis's money is sponsoring the next mayor?" Chloe asked.

The blood drained from Sikya's face.

Shada smiled. "You've caught on. Nothing happens in this city without WestCorp."

CHAPTER EIGHTEEN

RICHARD AND TONY showed up Saturday evening. They brought food with them: Chinese takeout, ice cream for dessert, and groceries for the next few days. They were both surprised to see Chloe there.

"We would have brought you," Tony said.

"It's OK, it was a last-minute thing." She didn't mention the business with Piper, and neither did the sisters. She tried to leave before the four of them ate dinner, but they convinced her there was enough food for all of them and she should stay for the meal.

"Just leave with us after dinner," Richard told her. "We'll give you a ride back."

Chloe agreed, and Sikya pulled out five plates. Tony opened containers of fried rice, lo mein, beef and broccoli, and cashew chicken and left them on the counter. Everyone took turns making a plate. Chloe, Shada, and Sikya sat at the kitchen table while Tony and Richard stood to eat.

During their meal, Chloe found out what the sisters had been up to to pass the time. Sikya had spent her days working on Tensen's campaign, cold-calling potential donors and following up with her contacts from the previous campaign. In the evenings she watched made-for-TV movies with Shada, low-budget romantic comedies. When Chloe asked Shada what she did while Sikya worked, Shada informed the group she was learning all she could about the history of WestCorp by combing through Hollis's memories.

"They've been busy through the years," Shada said. When asked by Richard to elaborate, she said there was nothing he needed to worry about at the moment.

"Well what about a future moment? Anything I need to know about then?"

Shada looked at him and in seriousness told him, "When you need to know, I'll tell you."

Richard's laugh didn't do much to cover his frustration.

Everyone helped clean up when the meal was over. The two men lingered for a while after, long enough for Chloe to get anxious about her trip back to the island for her nighttime dose of serum. Without probing Fisher's mind, she heard the mind inside her say he wouldn't try to take over her body.

"Look, the way I see it is we're stuck in here together. No reason to piss you off," Fisher gave as his reason.

Chloe still didn't trust him.

Richard's phone buzzed on the counter. After he picked it up and read the message, he looked at Tony and used his head to signal it was time for them to leave.

"We'll be back on Monday or Tuesday. Let us know if you need anything before then," Tony told the sisters.

Chloe hugged the sisters goodbye and left with the two men. She sat in the back seat, Richard in the front, and Tony drove into the city. Once the three of them were alone, Chloe told Richard that Alfie had agreed to perform the procedure on him.

"I was going to ask you about that," Richard said.

"I'll have to go over Shada's process to take back control," Chloe said. "It isn't the easiest thing to do."

"You can fill me in on the way to the island."

The way Richard said this planted the seed in Chloe's mind that they would be heading to the island together, but not at the current moment. When she looked out the window, she saw they weren't heading to the city's center. Instead, Tony was taking them to the eastern side of town, close to the water.

"Where are we going?" Chloe asked.

"You'll see," Richard said.

Chloe expected him to turn around and flash a smile, to let her know it was a pleasant surprise, but when he didn't, Chloe's mind turned towards darker possibilities. Could they be working for WestCorp as well? She kicked herself for not searching for their names in the employee files. Like Ruby had said, there were WestCorp employees all over the city. Could these be some of them?

Half an hour later, Tony pulled into a row of warehouses and parked outside the one farthest from the street. The massive parking lot was empty except for the spaces near their car, where there were a dozen or so other vehicles parked. Tony and Richard got out and told Chloe to come with them.

Chloe followed, grateful for the presence of other people. Her belief in their status as WestCorp employees had solidified in her mind, and when they arrived at the warehouse, she thought she would be interrogated. She couldn't figure out why they would go to such lengths, since she'd answered their every question right away, without lying, but her distrust of people forced her to prepare for the worst.

The door to the warehouse was up a set of metal steps to the left of a loading dock. She expected to see a massive space with high ceilings and concrete floors when she got inside. Instead, she found herself in a single room with a standard-height ceiling, the floors still concrete. She guessed a door opposite the door they'd entered led out to the warehouse. Chairs lined the walls of the room, and most of them were occupied by serious-looking individuals, all dressed in black and seeming to be in excellent physical shape.

Richard turned to Chloe. "These are all of my coworkers who are willing to receive uploads. We all work for Tensen," he said.

Each member of the group nodded. Chloe did a quick count and determined there were thirteen in total, including Tony and Richard.

"Alfie only agreed to upload a mind into you," Chloe said.

"And once that works, we can convince him to upload into everyone else. These are all highly trained, educated unedited. Imagine what we could do with the knowledge and resources an edited mind could provide."

"There would be a shift in power," Chloe said. It was a personal thought she shared out loud.

"We are the resistance," said a pretty brunette woman, her hair pulled back in a ponytail.

The group had the same agenda Chloe had advocated to Shada. Unedited humans capturing edited minds in order to both weaken WestCorp's position and increase the uniteds' power. Seeing it made real reminded her of Shada's desire to step away from the struggle and Sikya's insistence that uploads weren't the appropriate course of action. By being in the presence of a more radical group, Chloe was forced to adopt the stance of a moderate; in contrast, when she was in the presence of the more passive sisters, Chloe was transformed into the voice for action.

"We don't even know if uploading into you will work. Let's see how that goes," she said to Richard. She didn't like being the voice of reason.

"Why wouldn't it work?" Tony said. "You and Shada did it."

"We had already been uploaded into before. Both of us were able to see the world through our eyes while under control from another mind, Shada on the first upload and me on the fifth."

"We will learn to do it too."

"You're trying to run before you can crawl," Chloe said. She didn't mean to sound condescending, but being forced into action in front of the resistance made her lash out.

Richard's eyes read Chloe, and he took steps to defuse the situation. "She's right, let's see how my upload goes before we make plans for everyone else."

"What if you aren't the best possible candidate? It could fail for you but work for all of us," a large man with neck tattoos said.

It was Richard's turn to push back. "That's a risk we have to take. The scientist agreed to upload into me first."

The large man leaned to his side and grumbled to his neighbor.

"If you have something to say, say it to the group," Richard said, ice in his voice.

From the way the rest of the group watched the exchange, Chloe could tell the tension between these two had been seen before.

The man sat up straight in his chair. "I said they don't know what you look like. We could send any guy here and say he's Richard. Hell, any woman could be a Richard too, he doesn't know."

Tony jumped in. "Look, Richard's the one who got us this opportunity. Let's stick to the plan, and when his upload works, we can start the process of uploading into everyone else."

Chloe marveled at how her help in their plan was taken as a given.

Tony and Richard looked down at the seated man, and after a few tense moments he raised his hands in a display of surrender.

"Now let's move on to the reason for the meeting tonight," Richard said. "Does Tensen have any idea we're the ones who took care of the legislation?"

Fisher laughed, and Chloe knew she was right to assume the worst. These people were killers.

CHAPTER NINETEEN

Richard called an end to the meeting just before ten at night. The group filed out, leaving Tony, Richard, and Chloe behind. Richard and Chloe were first out the door, walking down the steps while Tony lingered behind to turn off the lights and lock the door behind them. Chloe wondered how many of the group's members had keys to the space.

"Want to stay in the city tonight and head back tomorrow?" Richard asked.

Chloe couldn't say no fast enough. "I need to get back to the island," she added, thinking of the vial of serum in her room.

Tony's eyes searched for Richard's response, and the leader nodded. They all climbed into the car and began the trip to the center of the city.

While the three passengers rode in silence, Chloe's personal passenger tried to convince her he wasn't worth worrying about. "I'm not going to try to take over," Fisher said in the space they alone had access to.

Chloe wasn't in the mood to argue. "I still don't trust you," she said to the voice in her head.

"When you take the serum, it feels like I'm turned upside

down," Fisher said, taking a different approach, trying to garner Chloe's sympathy. "I don't want to lose my view."

"Then you'd better remember how you found your sight in the first place. I'm not going to risk sleeping with you inside my head, able to take over while I'm unconscious."

"I could take over now," Fisher countered.

Chloe tensed up, searching every part of her body for signs of Fisher's control. After a few moments she realized it had been quite a while since she'd blinked. She focused and forced her eyelids to touch. "That wasn't funny," she said to Fisher.

"Relax, I am well aware you can negate any attempts I make."

Chloe didn't reply and let her awareness of Fisher fade.

"We need to make a quick stop," Richard informed Chloe.

"Quicker than the last stop, I hope," Chloe muttered. She had wanted to say, "It'd better be," but knew the threat would be meaningless. As long as she was in the car with them, she was at the mercy of their haphazard scheduling.

"It will be, I just need to grab my overnight bag. It's already packed," Richard said.

The extra stop made sense to Chloe, but it didn't mean she had to like it. It was one more thing delaying her nighttime injection, and without the serum, she had to stay more alert to her body in case Fisher tried to take another stab at control. She took a second to feel the breath entering her body and closed her eyes during her extended exhale.

Richard mistook her long breath as a sigh. "I promise it'll be quick. The meeting went longer than anticipated, sorry for that."

Chloe opened her eyes but didn't say a word.

Tony parked the car in front of a high-rise apartment building and turned on his hazard lights. Richard jumped out of the passenger seat and ran inside. He returned less than five minutes later with a black duffle bag slung over his shoulder.

"Told you it would be quick," he said, out of breath.

"Any longer and I would've walked," Chloe joked.

A few minutes later, Tony stopped outside the station.

Before Richard got out of the car, he grabbed Tony's forearm, and his colleague returned the gesture. The two of them locked eyes, their expressions saying what words could not. Chloe tried to climb out of the car in order to give their moment its space, but she wasn't fast enough, and the moment ended while she was still inside. Tony drove away when Richard and Chloe were on the sidewalk outside the station.

They paid to get into the city's train system then descended to the bottom level. The few people they passed on their way down appeared to be homeless, riding the rails and taking advantage of the indoors before spending the night out on the streets. The platform that hosted WestCorp's tram was dark and empty when the two of them arrived, but when they took their first steps onto its surface, lights began to pop on, starting at their location and extending off into the distance until the entire area was illuminated. A display screen came to life, telling the two of them the tram would be arriving in sixteen minutes.

Chloe assumed this was the exact time it took to travel to the island, that the tram had sensed their presence on the platform and deployed itself to pick them up. She sat down on a concrete bench with Richard and tapped the spot next to her, urging him to sit down. He said he preferred to stand.

"Well, we need to get you caught up with how you're going to take back control of your body," Chloe said. She went through the process of getting uploaded into, describing the room and equipment he would soon experience. Then she told him what it would feel like trapped in the darkness of his own mind.

"Like existing in the vacuum of space," she said.

Richard hung on to every word.

The empty tram arrived, and they climbed on. They sat down, and Chloe continued her lesson, telling him how to find his vision for the first time.

"Don't look right at it; it will disappear as soon as you try. Instead, look past it, around it, like trying to see a dim star. Let your peripheral vision see the dim light, and over time it will take over your vision." Part of Chloe hoped Fisher was listening, to help him after she took the serum.

Richard nodded, but Chloe had the sense he wasn't appreciating the nuance involved with this crucial step.

Chloe continued. "I'll be honest, I'm not sure when or how the hearing comes back. It just shows up when you can see the world through your own eyes again."

"Do you think it's possible to hear first?" Richard asked.

Chloe shook her head no. "The closest thing I can relate the experience to is floating to the top of a well. From the bottom, you can see the light, but the narrowness of the space makes it impossible to hear a thing. If you're patient, the light gets brighter, like you're getting closer to the top. Then, when you can see the world, it's like the sound is no longer being blocked by the well's walls."

"So the light from your eyes is the light at the top of the well? I have to float up from my feet?"

"In a way."

"Then the light should be off and to the side, not a single circle up top."

"Then think of it like your mind is a tiny dot in the back of your skull," Chloe said, reaching out and touching the back of Richard's head.

"Wouldn't there be two circles of light then?" Richard asked.

Chloe glared at him.

"What?" he said, taken aback.

"Ignore the metaphors, just remember the instructions. Wait for the light to take over your awareness, and you'll begin to hear the world around you."

The tram came to a stop beneath the island. Chloe, remembering the guards, grew concerned. "Do you have a gun on you?" she said.

"Of course," Richard replied.

"You'll be searched. Be ready to give it up."

Richard hesitated, then nodded. "That's fine. But they'd better give it back when I leave."

They walked off the tram and were stared down by the large humans posted on each side of the staircase leading up to the atrium. One of them held up a hand as they approached. "Stop," he said, his voice booming.

After they both obeyed, Chloe was waved forward. The guards gave no indication they remembered her, but their cursory search led her to believe they knew she wasn't a threat, by memory or instinct, she wasn't sure. Both guards participated in Richard's search. One withdrew a small computer and a knife from his duffel while the other took two pistols off his person, one from his side and one from his leg.

"These stay with us," the guard who searched the duffel said before shoving the lighter bag at Richard's chest.

With a look from Chloe, Richard nodded, and they both began climbing the steps.

CHAPTER TWENTY

CHLOE's personal transport vehicle was still parked where she had left it, outside the atrium. She climbed in first, holding Richard's bag on her lap as Richard climbed in. The vehicle was made for two, but the space was cramped. The trip to Chloe's room took no time at all, and the whole time she was imagining taking the serum. She injected herself as soon as she got into her room.

Richard, watching Chloe's face relax after the serum, asked what was in the vial. "Something Alfie made to help me make sure the mind inside doesn't take back control."

"It helps you see the light?"

"Not exactly," Chloe said. She sat down on her bed, and Richard leaned against the bathroom doorframe. She went on to explain the importance of finding the body's breath after seeing the light, how controlling it led to greater control of the entire body.

"And where does the serum come in?"

"It makes it possible to block the edited mind from taking back control." She twirled the empty vial between her fingers. "The serum allows you to sense your heartbeat resonating with the world around you. It's a much more powerful anchor than breathing."

"Why not just find your heartbeat without it?" Richard asked.

"Try it."

Richard stayed still. Chloe could see his breathing become regular and knew his heart rate would lower as a result.

"I just lowered my heart rate," Richard said with a smug grin. "They taught us how in training."

"The trick isn't lowering the heart rate. It's allowing it to resonate throughout your body so you can find every limb and maintain control. The serum allows us to do that while at the same time scrambling the edited mind inside."

Richard nodded. Chloe wondered if he was doing it to make her happy.

Chloe felt how tired she was after the conclusion of Richard's lesson. She informed him she was going to sleep. She appreciated that Richard assumed he was sleeping on the floor and as a reward gave him her comforter, despite his objections.

"I'm leaving it on the floor. Use it or not, it's up to you," she said.

In the darkness, with the serum coursing through her veins, she could sense the pulse of the world around her, including Richard's heartbeat. As she fell asleep, she felt him lower his heart rate on purpose before he was asleep, and she worried he had missed the point of the day's lesson.

Richard was already awake when Chloe rolled over the next morning and looked at him. He was staring at the ceiling.

"Morning," she said.

"Good morning," he replied without looking at her.

There was enough room next to her bed for Chloe to step off without Richard having to move, but she had to shuffle sideways in order to get to the rest of the room. Once she had more space, down near Richard's feet, she leaned back and stretched her back, cracking it twice in the process.

"Those were good," Richard said. Thin rays of light shone through the curtains, illuminating parts of his torso. His face was kept in shadow. He'd slept clothed and hadn't used the comforter, using his arm as a pillow instead.

A surge of guilt rose through Chloe when she saw the two pillows on her bed. She could have spared one, she just hadn't thought about it. She grabbed a vial of serum from the desk and took it into the bathroom to inject herself without Richard watching. He hadn't moved when she came out.

"So what's the plan?" Richard asked.

Chloe began to get dressed. "Well, Alfie doesn't know you're here, so I need to talk to him, tell him you're on the island."

Richard sat up. "And what am I supposed to do?"

"Whatever you want."

"Let me come with you. It'll be good for me to see the island."

"No, you need to keep a low profile."

"It's Sunday, nobody will give me a second look. I'll just act like an edited zombie."

"They aren't zombies," Chloe shot back. "If anything, they're happier than most. It's like a weird mix of aloofness combined with blind optimism."

"OK, I'll act like that then." Richard stood and opened the curtains. Sunlight poured into the room. He turned around with a wide grin pasted on his face.

Chloe couldn't contain her laughter. His expression went against everything she had come to expect. When she was able to talk again, she agreed to bring him to see Alfie, but they would have to come right back to the room afterwards.

"Deal," Richard said. This time, his thin-lipped smile was

genuine.

They took a moment to put the room back in order before they left. The transport vehicle, when told to bring them to Alfie, went to the lab. On their way, Chloe told Richard about the purpose of the buildings she knew and realized there were a lot more she had no idea about.

Richard seemed intrigued by the concept of a large space with rows of tables where post-birth edits were performed en masse on unedited humans. "They do them all at the same time?"

Chloe thought back to the pod Alfie had shown her in his personal lab, the one made for one human at a time. There was no way all the humans got edited on the tables, she realized.

"I think they are prepped in the large room then taken to a chamber where the edits actually take place," she said. "Piper said all those tables were for post-birth edits, but I guess she didn't feel like elaborating."

The transport stopped outside the lab, and the two of them climbed out. Chloe knew they would be stuck outside the entrance to the lab, since they didn't have the cards the scientists used to get past the locked doors, but she figured Alfie would be out to get them soon after being alerted to their presence.

They waited longer than expected.

While they waited, two scientists Chloe had never seen before swiped themselves into the lab. After the first one—a young woman with short hair—went in, Richard was about to try to catch the door behind her when Chloe put a hand on his arm to stop him. The scientist pulled the door shut. When the second scientist swiped himself in, Chloe asked in her most polite voice if the older man could tell Alfie he had someone waiting for him in the lobby. The scientist ignored her.

"Do people always work on Sundays?" Richard asked.

"I think a lot of their projects require daily attention. They probably take some extra time off during the week."

"Or just work all the time."

"Being artificially happy makes it easier, I'm sure."

No one entered or exited the lab for long enough that Chloe got nervous. Maybe Ruby had gotten wind Richard was there? Or Alfie had changed his mind about uploading the edited mind into Richard? Her stomach was in knots, and she got up to leave. She planned to take Richard back to her room and come back alone.

That was when Alfie came out with Ruby. Chloe stood up right away at the sight of her boss, and Richard followed her lead.

"So this is our second subject," the older woman said, looking at Richard with hungry eyes.

Chloe could feel Richard's eyes boring into the side of her head, searching for a clue about how to handle the current situation. She wanted to look at Alfie, to get a clue for herself, but doing so risked being witnessed by Ruby. She played along with Ruby instead. "This is him," she said.

Alfie placed a hand on Richard's shoulder. "You're brave for volunteering," the scientist said. His eyes were devoid of any emotion, a look Chloe found chilling. There wasn't even a hint of the happiness that was supposed to be edited into his mind.

"Thanks?" Richard said.

Alfie stepped aside and gestured for Richard to walk through the lab's doors. Chloe, still dazed from trying to figure out what was happening, tried to follow him, assuming she was going into the lab as well. Was this all part of Alfie's plan? Or had this been designed by Ruby?

"Chloe, can I have a word?" Ruby said, as if her assistant had any choice in the matter.

Alfie followed Richard into the lab and the door shut behind them, leaving Chloe and Ruby alone.

CHAPTER TWENTY-ONE

"Let's hope he can repeat what happened with Hollis and Shada."

Chloe's mouth dropped, betraying her disbelief at Ruby's open discussion on the topic. So Ruby knew about Shada but didn't know about Chloe, since she referenced Richard as the second subject.

"Oh, you didn't think I knew about that? About Michael's illness? The man doesn't have a body, I'd say that qualifies as an illness."

"That's why you had me kill Piper," Chloe whispered.

"And to prove yourself. Now that she's gone, I know where you stand."

Chloe's head spun trying to keep track of who knew what.

"The city will be looking for you soon, so it's time for you to move here permanently. I'll take you to your apartment in my personal helicopter to gather your belongings."

"I thought you said you'd convince them not to investigate me!" Chloe blurted out.

"I will, just give it a few days to die down. Right now, you need to get anything you want to keep out of your apartment."

Ruby led Chloe to the atrium, then through a series of tunnels that ended in a vast underground chamber. A black helicopter sat on a circular slab of concrete. A white circle was painted around the slab's edges, with a large white H painted in the middle. A crack in the middle of the roof above the chamber allowed a thin line of light to spill in. The two women climbed in, joining the pilot, who was already in the cockpit.

At a thumbs-up from the pilot, the helipad began to elevate. At the same time, light spilled into the chamber as the roof above opened. All motion stopped when the landing pad was level with the ground. The edge of the slab ended right at the start of the lawn around them. Without prior knowledge of the chamber, any onlookers wouldn't know about its existence below.

The pilot flipped a series of switches and the helicopter's rotors began to spin. Ruby handed Chloe a headset, telling her to put it on.

"Can you hear me?" Ruby said after placing her own headset over her ears.

Chloe nodded. She assumed the pilot could hear her too, but he didn't make any gesture to confirm.

The craft took flight, and Chloe felt a wave of butterflies in her stomach. She had never been in a helicopter before, and its rapid maneuvers unsettled her. They took off in the direction of the city.

When they were over the bay, Ruby began talking about her plan for the future direction of the company. "If Richard's upload is successful, we'll be able to give our senior employees a second life," she said. "Alfie said Shada was an anomaly."

Chloe stayed silent. At least Alfie knew for certain that Ruby was aware of Shada's procedure. She wasn't sure she wanted to know Alfie's plan for Richard. She had assumed he would help the unedited man take back control of his body from the edited mind, but the way Ruby talked, she wasn't sure whose side Alfie was on. The picture of Richard with his children flashed through her mind.

"Of course, we'll have to retrieve Shada when the time is right."

Chloe almost screamed that Ruby would never find Shada, but at the last second she remembered she was supposed to be edited. "She's still in the city, I'm sure."

"Does Richard know where she is?"

Ruby's straightforward question caught Chloe off guard. She decided not to lie. "He does."

"Good. Once he's been taken over, he can tell us where she is."

If Richard couldn't regain control, it would be a repeat of the Piper situation. Would she have to kill him too? It would be much harder than killing Piper. She shuddered at the memory of the loud thud of the woman's body against the front of the train.

Chloe wondered if Ruby ever thought about using her to find Shada.

Fisher crept into Chloe's awareness. "You're playing a dangerous game," he said. "Don't underestimate this woman."

Chloe blocked him out, knowing she needed to save her full attention for Ruby.

Ruby sighed. "Look at the city. So many unedited," she said with sadness, as if she was the sole person who cared about their future.

"There are a lot of them," Chloe replied. She kept her words about WestCorp being responsible to herself.

"Not for much longer, if I have anything to do with it."

"What do you mean?" Chloe asked.

"I'm going to offer free adaptations." The wrinkles at the corners of her lips deepened when she clenched her jaw.

Chloe was stunned. This would be an enormous cost to the company. "Free? Why?"

"To get rid of them," she snarled. "Filth like Shada have no place in the world I want to create."

"Will they all work for WestCorp?" Chloe asked.

"God no. I'm not editing them to become one of us. I'm going to edit them to become angry and impulsive. Then, I'll convince them that Shada has become the leader of WestCorp, that the negative edits were her, and Michael's, idea. It won't take long for them to rise up against her."

Chloe took a deep breath and reminded herself she was supposed to be happy. She smiled. "Then why bother trying to find her with Richard?"

"So I can tell the unedited hordes where to find her! I'll make sure they know what she looks like before letting them loose," Ruby said. Her wicked smile came with a dash of pride.

Chloe forced herself to smile back. When she looked out the window, she recognized the area of the city they were over. "We're close," she said.

Ruby looked out the window. "You live here?"

"Lived," Chloe corrected.

The pilot landed the helicopter on top of Chloe's building. Chloe began to climb out, and Ruby made no sign she would be joining.

"Make it quick. Ten minutes, tops," Ruby said.

Chloe exited the helicopter and rushed across the roof. The door to the roof had been broken as long as Chloe could remember; it hung loose on its hinges and never shut. She threw it open and took the stairs two at a time down to her floor. She surveyed her room once inside. It was just how she'd left it except for the plants, which had succumbed to neglect, their leaves brown and withered. She almost took the time to water them but knew it would be a waste of time.

She went to the closet, retrieved several large bags she used for groceries, and began stuffing clothes inside. It seemed pointless since WestCorp provided the island's inhabitants with uniforms, but she didn't plan on staying there forever. She looked at the spot where the framed photo of her grandfather once stood and remembered it was in her bag on the island. It had been too long since she'd seen his face, and she didn't want to forget her ultimate goal, to leave the city behind and live in a house in the country, far away from this mess. The items she wanted most, the vials of poison and antidote created by her mother, she withdrew from her safe and stuffed into the pockets of a pair of jeans. By returning to the island on the helicopter, she wouldn't have to get them past the guards. She left the safe open so anyone searching her room wouldn't have to bother opening it.

There were a few toiletries Chloe wanted from the bathroom, and some books, like 1984 and Catcher in the Rye, that she had kept for so long she couldn't imagine not owning them, so she grabbed these and put them into the bags as well.

Chloe took one last look at the plants in her room, her surrogate family, and regretted breaking her promise to be back before they wilted. She turned away from them before she got emotional. "Edited humans are always happy," she reminded herself.

With the bags in hand, Chloe left her apartment behind.

Ruby beckoned for Chloe to hurry across the roof when she was in sight of the helicopter. Chloe walked as fast as she could without running.

"You have everything?" Ruby asked when Chloe climbed up and sat down, her bags on the floor by her feet.

Chloe told her she did.

Ruby pulled out her phone and sent a message as the helicopter ascended. She saw Chloe looking at her phone and explained. "I just informed the authorities you were a suspect in Piper's murder. They'll be at your place soon."

"They didn't know yet?" Chloe yelled. She was furious.

"Relax, you won't be a suspect for long. I'll make sure whatever evidence they collect gets misplaced. I just needed you on the island permanently."

Chloe took several deep breaths. Fisher reminded her Ruby was a snake. "She'll bite you the first chance she gets."

"For now, you can't go back into the city. But there's plenty to do on the island," Ruby said.

"They can't come get me there?"

Ruby laughed. "On my island? No way! It's part of our deal."

Chloe couldn't believe the situation WestCorp had created for themselves. At first, she marveled at Ruby, but she knew Michael was the real architect. She was both impressed and scared of the power the company wielded.

They were over the bay when Ruby told Chloe about her new role. "Every morning, I need you to meet with the new unedited recruits. Make sure they feel welcome, answer any questions they have, and get them into staging before their edits."

Chloe grew nauseous at the thought. "Similar to the role Piper filled when I first arrived . . ." she reminisced.

"Whose fault is it she won't be there to perform her duties?" Ruby said, one eyebrow raised.

Chloe squeezed her lips together for a moment, resigning herself to her fate. "Have the free edits already begun?" she asked.

"They are set to begin tomorrow. Your first day of work!"

CHAPTER TWENTY-TWO

CHLOE WAITED in the atrium for the first wave of unedited humans from the city to arrive. She had been informed by Ruby that she was to take care of the recruits in the morning then go to Ruby's office in the afternoon to complete her personal assistant work. The long hours expected of her loomed over her like a dark cloud, and she knew Ruby wasn't the type of person to cut Chloe's workday short because of her increased responsibility. In the city, Chloe would have refused to comply, or at the very least voiced her displeasure, but part of being edited was supposed to be the feeling of happiness, regardless of the situation. Knowing this, she did her best to paste a smile on her face and settle into the long days ahead.

She had made a sign and placed it on a stand right above the stairs, telling the people coming to the island for edits to walk to the left and sit down in a sectioned-off portion of the seating area. Instead of waiting inside the area herself, she stayed back, near a restaurant, so she could watch the people she had to deal with before they knew she was in charge.

The first arrivals climbed the steps, their eyes wide with awe. They stopped in front of the sign then followed its instructions, taking seats at separate tables. As more people emerged from the platform, they had to sit down at tables already occupied, engaging in small talk while they waited. Chloe waited a few minutes after the last arrivals sat down before approaching. Her stomach was in knots knowing these people had been tricked into getting edits that could make their lives more difficult, that their edits wouldn't bring about the positive changes they hoped.

"Welcome to WestCorp!" she said as she walked up, loud enough for everyone to hear and with as much command as she could muster. A script hadn't been provided for her. "We are honored you chose to trust us with your future."

There were murmurs of greeting from the crowd. One of the men seated in the middle of the group looked at a woman by his side, his eyes telling her how upset he was to be there, before she elbowed him in the ribs. She tapped his leg twice as an olive branch.

"Now, if you'll follow me . . ." Chloe said.

The island's visitors all stood up and lined up behind the space in the partition.

Chloe led the group out the back entrance, the same path she'd taken with Shada. It felt like forever ago. Somehow, the transit system on the island knew to provide a larger transport vehicle, and one the size of a bus sat waiting for the group of new arrivals. Nobody thought twice about the absence of a driver, and as soon as the last member of the group sat down, the bus began to move.

It took less than five minutes to arrive at the warehouse. The group was quiet except for the few whispered, private conversations of people who'd come to the island together. Chloe, in the front seat, informed them they had arrived when the bus stopped outside the warehouse. She stood outside the door of the bus as everyone climbed off, then took a look inside to make sure everyone had disembarked. There was a solitary woman in the back seat, tears streaming down her face. Chloe walked back and sat down in the seat next to her.

"I can't do it," she said.

"Come on now, we're already here," Chloe said, drawing on all the sweetness she possessed.

"I left my kids with my mother. I was convinced I was doing the right thing, creating a future for my children. But now I can't help but think I'm abandoning them!" The woman didn't cry out, but tears streamed down her face anew.

Chloe sat, waiting for the woman to continue. Pretending to be edited was hard, but pretending she wasn't one of them, unedited, was harder. She wanted to take this woman under her wing, to tell her there were steps being taken to topple the company for good, to help this woman as well as unburden her own mind.

"It's for the best," the woman said after a deep breath, finding her resolve. She nodded as if convincing herself of the fact. "For the best," she repeated.

"It is," Chloe said. Her skin crawled at how easy it was for her to help WestCorp manipulate the unedited.

The woman stood and walked off the bus, joining the people milling about outside the warehouse. Chloe, having joined the crowd, stood on tiptoes and called out, "This way, everyone!"

Inside the warehouse were rows of stainless steel tables. There were enough to accommodate many more than were with her, so she told the cohort to each take a table but bias towards the front of the room. "There will be more people joining you shortly," she yelled out. "Please be patient. Bathrooms are in the back"—she pointed to the far wall—"and there is reading material present near the door we entered through. Please don't try and leave the premises, or the alarm will sound and you'll be escorted back by security. I can't guarantee you won't be restrained."

Chloe searched the faces, trying to determine if anyone else would get cold feet. The crying woman appeared resolute. "Any questions?" Chloe asked.

The husband who'd given his wife a look raised his hand and began to speak without being acknowledged. "How many more people will there be?"

"I've been informed there are three waves coming in today. So, most of these tables will be filled before we begin." The group looked at the empty tables around them, and Chloe took their distraction as her opportunity to leave.

She rode the bus back alone and walked into the atrium to find a group already waiting for her. WestCorp ran like clockwork. She repeated the procedure twice more and left the warehouse for the final time that day with most of the tables full, just like she'd said.

When Chloe returned to the atrium for the final time, she raced to the bathroom and washed her hands. She stared at her face in the mirror for a long time, disgusted at herself for helping WestCorp. She felt Fisher try to communicate with her, but she blocked off his access to her, not wanting to deal with the edited mind. She was angry at the edited, and she lumped the mind inside her body along with them even though he'd had no involvement in the distribution of the free negative edits.

She walked out of the bathroom, intent on getting food before starting the second half of her day, but stopped short when she saw Richard.

He was wearing the WestCorp business uniform, a white polo and khaki pants, and walked around the food court as if seeing it with fresh eyes, a newfound appreciation for the world around him. She knew without speaking to him the edited mind was still in control.

"It's only been a day," she told herself. She closed her eyes and focused on her breath. She wanted to follow Richard but knew it was no use. He had no idea who she was.

Fisher, in the background, told her to stop worrying about him. "And Shada, for that matter. They'll be fine," he said.

"Be quiet," she thought, focusing on her exhale.

"If your goal is to live outside the city alone, it doesn't make sense to forge ties with people. You'll have to walk away from them eventually; just stop caring now so it isn't so hard," Fisher said.

Chloe tried to lie and tell Fisher she didn't care about Richard but wasn't able to silence her true thoughts. If she had to lie with her words, she could've done it, but thinking a lie, hiding it from herself, wasn't something she was able to do.

"I knew it," Fisher said.

Chloe walked in the opposite direction to Richard, in search of food. "You should be worried too," Chloe said to Fisher inside her mind.

"And why is that? He isn't my friend."

"If Richard tells anyone about your upload into my body, we'll both be in trouble. It's not like you have a body you can go back into."

Fisher was quiet while Chloe purchased a bar and a smoothie from the coffee shop. She devoured them both with minimal time spent breathing. She began the walk to Ruby's office.

"Realistically, what can they do to me? My body is already dead, so what if my mind goes too. But you . . ."

Chloe stopped in the hallway, waiting for Fisher to continue.

"They could put your mind into a different body and kill you. Then I'd have free reign." Fisher twitched Chloe's thumb, and Chloe, instead of stopping him, allowed it to continue.

"I'd never leave my own," she said.

"You wouldn't have a choice."

Chloe knew Fisher was bluffing. Every upload had to be voluntary, or else there wouldn't be complete transference. It was part of the briefing Alfie had gone through with Fisher before his own upload. Chloe's access to his memories made it so Fisher couldn't sustain any deception for long.

"It's only been a day," she repeated to herself, hopeful Richard had been paying attention when she'd told him how to find the light.

CHAPTER TWENTY-THREE

CHLOE FOUND Ruby luxuriating in her office, her feet on the desk and head resting on the top of her leaned-back chair, staring at the ceiling. The head of WestCorp didn't move when Chloe entered.

"How was it?" she asked.

Chloe pasted a smile on and reported her first day in her new assignment had been "wonderful."

"Did you need something from me?" Ruby asked.

"No, just wanted to let you know I arrived."

"Noted. Shut the door on your way out," Ruby said.

Chloe retreated and shut the door behind her. She cursed the older woman under her breath, then cursed herself for sticking around when she wanted to leave, the rebellious streak in her coming out. There wasn't any work for her to do. Instead of turning on her computer and pretending to work, she stared at her reflection and descended into Fisher's memories, looking for previous interactions he'd had with Ruby.

The two of them had never had direct contact with each other. The memories Chloe could find were times when Ruby was present in the front of a room as Michael's wife, smiling and seeming to agree with everything the previous leader of West-Corp said. Ruby once spoke by herself to Fisher's team, a few dozen people, outlining the importance of their work and thanking them for a job well done. The memory was infused with a sense of gratitude because the group had had minimal recognition from the leaders of the company. This time, they were thanked for their ability to organize a massive influx of candidates for editing, the first time the company had rolled the service out to the public, and Fisher's group had worked day and night to get the work complete. The warehouse filled with stainless steel tables had come from this project.

Chloe stumbled on the memory of a rumor from a time before Michael and Ruby were married. They had been selected for each other—or rather he'd selected her—but there were rumblings within the company that Ruby's family had poisoned her name. Ruby's father had run away from the island, leaving his wife and a young Ruby behind, to go into the city and be with an unedited woman. This was before WestCorp had their current reach, and there was nothing the company could do. They'd kept tabs on him, plotting how they could get back at the man. The whole company was aware of the trajectory of his life; Fisher couldn't remember if the company told everyone or word got out through loose lips. Either way, they found out when he became mayor of the city. This news was the last Fisher had heard of Ruby's father. By then, Michael had ignored the members of WestCorp who disagreed with his selection and married Ruby. From then on, WestCorp had been involved with every major election, making sure their preferred candidates were the ones elected.

A siren rang out, pulling Chloe out of Fisher's memory. She now knew why Ruby hated the unedited so much: they had almost cost her a future.

The siren didn't stop. It was earsplitting and seemed to

come from every corner of the room. Chloe questioned Fisher about what it meant.

"Emergency," he said. "You need to exit the building."

Chloe jumped up and walked into Ruby's office without a second thought. "What's going on?" she yelled, loud enough for her boss to hear.

Ruby was in the same position Chloe had left her and showed no signs of moving. "No idea," she said with a shrug. Her words came in a space between siren blares.

"Do we need to leave?" Chloe asked.

Ruby didn't move. "I'm not going anywhere. Go find out what this is about, then come back and tell me."

Chloe didn't know how she heard Ruby's words over the noise of the siren. "What if it's a fire?" Chloe asked. Part of her was impressed by the woman's nonchalance.

"That's a different alarm."

Chloe shrugged. "Good to know. I'll be back." She shut the door behind her when she left.

Years of fire drills as a child had made Chloe associate loud indoor sirens with leaving the building, so she found the nearest exit and walked out into the sunlight. There were other people outside, all streaming to the left, towards another side of the building. The same siren seemed to be blaring from every adjacent building, but outside, the noise wasn't so overwhelming. She caught the sound of her heavy breathing, took a moment to calm down, and followed the crowd.

Chloe turned the corner and saw the backs of a large group of people. There was a space near the center of the mass enclosed by the semicircle of people and the wall. On the opposite side of the space, emergency services forced their way through the crowd, towards what everyone was gathered around. Chloe had never seen people wearing this uniform, but their dark shirts, matching dark baseball caps, and commanding air made it obvious they were there to take care of the situation. When they made it to the center of the crowd, their hats disappeared as they ducked down to inspect the source of the commotion.

It seemed every person but Ruby had exited the building. The crowd swelled, and more people came from surrounding buildings. Within minutes, Chloe was near the center of the mass. She searched the sea of faces, hoping to see Richard. If she could get near him and talk to him, she could find out if he had been able to switch. Maybe she could find her own heartbeat and allow it to resonate with his. She thought of Shada, knowing her friend would be the one who could pull off a maneuver like that with so many people around; there was a massive chance noise would be introduced to the experiment. But she could try.

She worked her way forward, keeping her eyes on the faces across from her, looking for Richard. She got to the open space, looked down, and found what she was looking for.

His body was bent in awkward, rigid angles, reminding Chloe of a cubist painting. His ear rested on his shoulder, and there was a space between the bones of his neck where two corners of broken bone pushed against the skin. It struck her how important that space was, how it signified his death more than the blood running down from his mouth.

"He jumped," a woman told the two men and the woman with dark baseball caps. "And landed just like that."

"We heard," one of the dark hats replied.

The sirens stopped blaring, but the voices of the crowd took their place as an incessant noise, a constant buzzing in Chloe's head. She turned and walked away, numb, making it back to Ruby's office without realizing where she was going until she arrived.

"What happened?" Ruby asked when her door was opened.

"The second upload test was a failure."

Ruby sat up. "How do you know?"

"He just jumped off a roof. He's dead outside." Chloe stared at the rolling waves in the distance through Ruby's window on the back wall.

"Damn," Ruby said. She looked down and away, thinking. "We'll need to run another test."

Chloe remembered Richard's children and a wave of nausea swept over her. She dreaded putting another life at risk.

"Alfie better get it right this time," Ruby said.

"Agreed," Chloe said, and she meant it. There was no reason for anyone else to die.

Ruby stood up and looked out her window, blocking the bay from Chloe's view. "I know he's using Michael's underground bunker as another lab, but he doesn't know I know." She turned around with a grin on her face. "I monitor the electricity usage of the space," she said.

Chloe appreciated Alfie's caution when forging her edits, how he'd run the machine just to consume the electricity. The man knew what he was talking about.

"I need to keep him around long enough to perfect the process. I wonder if he botched this one on purpose . . ." she said. She shook her head no. "No, he wants this to succeed as much as I do. He wouldn't."

Chloe stayed silent, marveling at the stream of Ruby's thoughts.

"I'll need to replace him eventually though. I can't have someone on the island working behind my back, even if he's my son." Ruby leaned on her desk and tapped her fingers. She looked at Chloe. "What would you do if someone took away the person you loved?"

Chloe guessed where Ruby's mind was headed and wanted to get to her conclusion first. "Do you want me to kill Alfie?" she asked. Although she was still numb from seeing Richard's dead body, she was surprised at how her question didn't come with any emotions. Maybe being around the edited had made her less emotional even without going through the procedure.

"No, if anything I'll send him to the city. We still need him for now. We just need to keep in mind that he has an agenda of his own. Can't give him too much power until we find out what it is."

Chloe nodded and, after asking if Ruby needed anything else, excused herself. She was amazed the woman didn't realize Chloe had her own agenda as well.

CHAPTER TWENTY-FOUR

"Ruby wants to get rid of you," Chloe told Alfie in his office. It was night, and she was exhausted from her first day filling two roles in the company. She'd willed herself to come see the scientist, to talk to him, even though she wanted to curl up in bed and sleep. Seeing Richard's dead body on the lawn had strengthened her resolve.

Alfie sat back before looking up and to the left. His eyes returned to Chloe. "She does, does she? And what makes you say that?"

"She told me herself."

"And did she share her reasons why?"

"Wants to get back at you for uploading Michael into Shada."

Alfie smiled. "Well, I'm right here."

"She won't do it until you have the chance to upload an edited mind without the unedited host taking back over."

"It seems I was close. Richard must have been worried he wouldn't take back over for good, even with the serum, and decided to jump off the building instead of being trapped inside."

Chloe shifted in her seat. "If he was able to get that bit of control, why not try again later? The first bit of control is the hardest."

"Maybe he realized he was in over his head. Or he didn't like the sensation of losing control of his body. For someone like him, it had to be unsettling."

"Has there been any news about him telling anyone that I was uploaded into as well?" Chloe asked. She didn't want to say his name; referring to Richard as "him" was more tolerable.

"I was going to ask you the same thing. Did Ruby receive any news while you were there?"

"I was only there for the second half of the day; the first half was spent guiding unedited recipients of the free edits to the warehouse where their procedure would take place."

Alfie thought for a moment. "Did Ruby act weird at all?"

"Very. She was staring at the ceiling and didn't move for a very long time. Now that I think about it, she could have been digesting the information, deciding what to do having found out about Fisher in my body."

Chloe felt Fisher's awareness spike at the mention of his name.

Alfie let the revelation settle before offering his thoughts. "Without definitive proof Richard was able to take over, it's hard to believe the edited mind even thought to probe his memories. Even if it was considered, and attempted, it's my guess Richard was still too deep to access. I'd guess your secret is safe, but we need to monitor Ruby closely to make sure she doesn't have any idea about you."

The scientist's logic seemed sound to Chloe, and she felt better after hearing his assessment.

"I do have something for you," Alfie said. "Richard gave it to me before his upload." He opened one of his desk drawers, withdrew the picture of Richard with his children, and handed it to

Chloe. "He said if anything happens to him, he wants this to get back to his family."

Chloe's hand shook as she accepted the photo. She avoided looking at it and put it in her pocket. "I can't go into the city right now, the authorities are looking for me in connection with Piper's murder."

Alfie didn't bat an eye; he must have known she was the one who killed her. "Ruby told me you were involved. Said the edits worked well when I met with her yesterday."

"Is that all you two talked about? I was furious when I saw her walk out of the lab with you."

"Among other things. She came right out and said she knew I'd uploaded Hollis into Shada. I thought she'd be more upset than she was, but it sounds like she's taking time to set up her revenge."

"She's a snake," Fisher said to Chloe. Chloe relayed the sentiment to Alfie without attributing it to the edited mind inside her.

"Too calculating for her own good, I'd say. If she just came out and told me what she wanted, I could help her."

"You'd help her get rid of you?"

"Well, maybe not, then," Alfie said with a smile. "But even if she took away my access to the lab, I could continue working in Hollis's bunker."

"She knows about the underground lab too."

Alfie shook his head and cursed under his breath.

"What else did you two discuss in your meeting?" Chloe asked.

"Not much else. She said she wanted to perfect the process of uploading, and that's when I told her about the next test we would be doing, on Richard. She seemed pleased to hear I was already working on the project. The whole thing was rather quick. And unexpected. She just showed up."

"So you're trying to make it so the unedited mind can't regain control of their own body? Am I and Shada going to be the only two who end up this way?" Chloe said. She felt her blood pressure rise.

Alfie leaned forward in his chair. "I could lie to you and tell you no, that I'm on your side, trying to allow the unedited to take over edited minds. But the truth is that I want to be able to do both successfully."

Chloe glared at the man.

"You have to understand. I'm a scientist. If I told you it didn't bother me that my initial hypothesis was incorrect, I'd be lying."

Chloe stood up. "Were you trying to make it so Fisher would take over my body?" she yelled.

Alfie asked Chloe to sit back down. "No point in getting worked up," he said.

She sat down and crossed her arms, waiting for the scientist to continue.

"Truth be told, I didn't know what was going to happen. I had to try again, repeat the conditions of the first experiment and record the results. It's not like I can run large trials of this procedure. I had a feeling you would be able to take back control, but I wasn't sure."

"Shada's the only reason I was able to. If she didn't tell me how to do it, I doubt I'd have figured it out."

"Well, the process didn't work for Richard. I'm assuming you told him the same steps to take."

"I did."

"And now we know there's something else required. Maybe it's because you are both female and he was a male? I could test it on another male, see if I can get the same results. But in an ideal world, I'd test two males, one with instructions from you and one from Shada, seeing if the instructions are the differentiator. Then, your history with uploads comes into play. Did your prior experience with the uploads set you up for success when the stakes were higher? What about Shada allowed her to take control after her first upload? Is one upload sufficient prior experience?"

Chloe's head spun trying to keep track of the possibilities, and she informed Alfie that she understood the point.

"So what I'm after is repeatable results. Science is what matters to me. The mind that ends up in control at the end of the day is just data to be analyzed."

While Chloe didn't like Alfie's uncaring attitude about the people involved, she did appreciate the dedication to his work.

"There is one question I'm dying to find the answer to . . ." Alfie said. He seemed hesitant.

"What?"

"If it's possible to capture multiple minds in the same body."

Chloe thought for a moment. Fisher said he thought it was possible right away. "If the person in charge of the body could keep them organized," he said in Chloe's mind, "I think it could be done. Not sure how much access everyone would have though."

"Fisher said he thinks it's possible. It'd have to be Shada," Chloe told Alfie.

Alfie's eyes betrayed his curiosity.

Chloe continued. "Do you have an edited candidate in mind? Maybe someone who wouldn't be too much to handle?"

"I do have someone I'd test in an ideal world, but they'd be a handful." After a pause, he said, "What if we got Ruby and Michael back together?"

Chloe laughed, then, when she realized Alfie was serious, her jaw dropped.

"Shada wouldn't have to worry about Ruby trying to kill Hollis once and for all, and Ruby would be out of our hair."

"Who would take over WestCorp?" Chloe asked, wondering if this was Alfie's attempt at taking over the company himself.

"Shada, in possession of Michael and Ruby Hollis," he said without hesitation. "The whole world would find out what WestCorp is capable of."

"If the world doesn't turn on you first. Ruby's free edits are to make the city's inhabitants angry and impulsive; once word gets out, the city will clamor for retribution."

"They'll come for the one who designed them," Alfie said, his head lowering. He had accepted his fate. "That's also what we were discussing yesterday. She wanted to make sure they were ready."

Chloe could have jumped across the desk and strangled the man. "You're helping her!"

"I had to prove my loyalty. You of all people should understand the importance of that."

CHAPTER TWENTY-FIVE

"Mrs. Hollis?" Chloe said from the door to her boss's office. It was Friday, the end of a long week of corralling unedited newcomers to the warehouse every morning.

Ruby took a moment to respond, choosing to finish reading her computer screen before acknowledging her assistant. When her eyes did find Chloe, she seemed to be far away, as if she had something else on her mind.

"Have you told the police to stop investigating me for Piper's death?" Chloe asked.

"No, I meant to do it yesterday. I'll take care of it." She looked back at her computer monitor, trying to end their conversation.

Chloe wasn't done. "Could you make sure you do it before tomorrow? I need to go back into the city."

Ruby didn't hesitate on her screen this time. "Into the city? What for?"

"Richard, the second test, had a picture he wanted returned to his family. Alfie gave it to me to bring back to them."

"A picture of what?"

Her gut reaction was to ask her boss why it mattered, but she humored the curious woman instead. "Of him and his two children."

Ruby shook her head. "Sentimental nonsense. Go, if you must."

Chloe wasn't asking permission. She had never been told she was expected to work on the weekends, so she felt that time was hers to use as she saw fit. She just had to make sure she wasn't going to be arrested before she went.

"So you'll take care of the police today?" Chloe asked.

"Yes, I'll take care of it today. If for whatever reason you are stopped, you can always just tell them you live on the island. Working for WestCorp has its benefits."

Chloe marveled at Ruby's confidence. She wanted to believe her, to think the company gave her a sort of immunity, but her years spent in the city, seeing the way the police targeted the underprivileged, made her doubt the effectiveness of this protection.

Ruby finished work late on Friday night, and Chloe had to sit at her desk with nothing to do until after the sun had gone down. She skipped dinner and went straight to bed, exhausted from the week and wanting to have a full night's rest for her trip. She woke up on her own on Saturday, groggy.

Her trip into the city was uneventful. The policemen at the city's transportation hub didn't give her a second look. It was a relief to stop pretending she was happy all the time now that she was off the island, and her face reverted to a neutral, borderline unapproachable look.

Chloe had no idea where Richard's family lived, so she went to the Office of Unedited Rights, hoping Tensen or someone else there could provide her with more information. The building had bare-bones security and was otherwise empty.

Chloe walked into Tensen's office and found it in the process of moving. Boxes were piled near the door, and movers were filling more. Tensen recognized Chloe when she walked in and came right over to her when she arrived.

"You're moving?" Chloe asked.

"To the mayor's office. It became official yesterday," Tensen said with a smile.

"Congratulations!" Chloe said. It was easy to slide back into pretending to be happy when in reality she didn't care.

"What brings you in?" Tensen asked.

"I need to find Richard's family. Do you know where they live?"

Tensen's eyes narrowed. "Not offhand, but I can find out. Why? Did something happen to him?"

Chloe informed the now-mayor that Richard was dead, leaving out the part where an edited mind had been uploaded into his body. Tensen's remorse knocked him sideways, causing him to put one hand on his barren desk for support.

"When did it happen?"

"Monday," Chloe replied.

Tensen shook his head. "First they roll out the free edits without telling us, now they don't report when a resident dies on their island. Seems they're trying their hardest to end our relationship."

Chloe wanted to remind the mayor the deal had been made with snakes, to not be surprised when he got bit, but she kept her mouth shut.

"Do you know where his wife and children live?"

"Ex-wife, if I remember correctly. Why?"

"Richard wanted me to give them something. A picture he carried with him."

Tensen nodded. "Understood. Let me find out."

Tensen waved away a mover who was about to unplug the computer, stopping him just in time. After some typing, he printed out the address and asked Chloe if she could inform them of Richard's passing. "It would save me the trouble of bothering them twice," he explained.

Chloe thought bother wasn't the best choice of words but agreed to tell them. She wished Tensen good luck in his new position before saying goodbye.

"Let me know if you need anything else," Tensen called out to her as she left.

Chloe kept walking, trying to determine how she would ever be able to contact the mayor of the city in the event she did need anything else. She was convinced he said that to everyone, always looking to gather votes.

A car accident had just occurred outside the building. There was a police officer in the street, directing traffic to go around the two vehicles involved. Meanwhile, the drivers of the vehicles were arguing about who was at fault. A crowd was beginning to gather on the far side of the street, watching the incident unfold. Seeing all this, Chloe realized how much she missed the city and its chaos.

At a break in the traffic the police officer looked right at her. He seemed to recognize her and put his hand to the radio clipped on his uniform.

Chloe's heartbeat quickened, and Fisher brought himself to the forefront. "Bet Ruby didn't bother to tell the police to end the investigation," he said. "Shouldn't have trusted her." If he had a head to shake, it would be moving left to right.

"Shut up," Chloe thought. She could have blocked him out but didn't want to put forth the effort. She assumed more police officers were already on their way and knew she had a limited amount of time before they showed up. She turned away and heard the officer yell for her to stop. Her rebelliousness peaked, and she thought about how, for the second time in a span of minutes, a man had yelled at her back, telling her what to do, as she walked away. A surefire way to make sure whatever it was they wanted never happened.

She didn't stop, continuing through the building she'd just left and leaving through a back exit. She began running to the closest train station a few blocks away.

"Not suspicious at all," Fisher said.

Chloe laughed to herself, appreciating his sarcasm. "They're showing up for an accident. I'm just a lonely woman late for an appointment," she said, in her mind, to Fisher. Thinking this made Chloe believe it herself, and her facial expression was one of someone who was exasperated at themselves for running late yet again.

"Sorry to burst your bubble, but if they did send out a report that you were here, they'll be looking for you," Fisher said.

Chloe ran faster.

Inside the train station, she looked at the address. She referenced her phone and found out it was a few stops before Shada's hideout. Keeping an eye out for officers, and avoiding the station's employees, she boarded the next train in that direction. She kept her head down against the seat in front of her, looking at her feet, risking a quick look at each stop to see who got on the train and if any of them were looking for her.

Chloe got off the train and called a car to take her to the address she'd been given. The houses she passed were small, a front door and a few small windows wide, packed together so tightly there couldn't have been much privacy from the neighbors. The car pulled up to her destination, a run-down single-family house similar to the others except for a single-car garage, which seemed to take up too much of the house's total space.

There were bikes lying on the tiny patch of grass and an assortment of balls by the front door. Three different scooters leaned against the garage door, all the same height; Chloe guessed there were other kids living in one or more of the houses nearby. She thanked the driver and got out of the car.

She stood in front of the house, wondering what to say. She remembered when she'd found out her mother died, when her grandfather had told her she would be raised by her dad. She was young and didn't appreciate the significance at the time. It wasn't until later in life that her father told her that her mother had committed suicide because she was blacklisted and couldn't find anywhere to continue her research. She hoped her dad was happy, wherever he was.

"Where'd he go?" Fisher asked. This was the first time Chloe had felt violated by his presence.

Fisher sensed Chloe's anger and asked her how it felt.

"I'll learn to deal with it," Chloe said. "And I haven't heard from him since he went down south to live near the water."

When the front door opened, Chloe realized she had been standing in front of the house for far too long. A pretty young woman with disheveled hair stood in the doorway, a quizzical look on her face. Chloe approached and said she had news about Richard.

"He's dead, isn't he?" the woman asked.

"Yes," Chloe said. She appreciated the directness of Richard's former partner. "He wanted me to give you and the children this." Chloe handed over the photo.

The woman took a look at it, holding it for a long moment. Chloe didn't think her time was spent reminiscing; rather, it looked like the woman couldn't decide whether to tear the photo up in pieces now or keep it to throw away later.

"He never should have gotten mixed up with those edited bastards," she snarled.

Chloe nodded.

"I told him, don't poke them or they'll strike out. That's why I left him in the first place: I knew I couldn't depend on him."

A young boy and a girl ran from upstairs, past the front door and out the back. A larger boy who was chasing them stopped at the front door and looked at Chloe. "Who are you?" he asked, curious.

"Came to give us this," his mother said. She shoved the photo in his hand.

The boy looked at the photo before shoving it in his pocket.

"What do you say?" his mother said to him.

"Thanks," he said. An automatic answer.

Chloe wondered what the boy's mother had told him about his father.

"Do you need anything else?" the woman asked Chloe.

Chloe looked at the boy, ignoring his mother. "I'm going to get the person who did this to your dad." She wished someone had told her the same thing when she was younger.

The mother pushed him away. "Go play with the others."

The boy stared at Chloe before leaving. His mother glared at Chloe before closing the door in her face.

Chloe walked away, confused. The interaction with Richard's family hadn't been what she'd expected and, worse, had stirred up emotions she had long since buried. Before she got far from the house, she heard a small voice call out for her to wait. She turned around and saw the boy running towards her, the picture still in his hands. She knelt down.

"Will you take care of the bad people? That's what dad said he was going to do."

Chloe nodded. "I'm going to get rid of them."

"Good," the boy said. He stood still for a moment then ran up to her, gave her a hug, and ran away.

Fisher hadn't missed the exchange. "How are you going to do that?" he asked.

"I'm going to take over every edited mind on that island."

"You want another Richard? Their blood will be on your hands."

Chloe thought for a moment. "I need to talk to Shada."

CHAPTER TWENTY-SIX

CHLOE RANG the bell and stood in the middle of the driveway, in front of the gate, so the sisters could see it was her outside their safe house. She looked around, paranoid a random officer could be passing by. It wasn't long before she heard a buzz and the gate slid to the left, allowing her to pass. As soon as she was through, it began closing, not ever getting far enough open for a car to pass through. The front door was thrown open as she walked up.

"Sorry to barge in on you like this," Chloe said.

"Don't say sorry! We're glad to have you," Sikya said in the doorway. She stepped aside and allowed Chloe to enter, closing the door and following her into the kitchen. Shada stood up from the kitchen table, crossed the room, and gave her friend a hug.

When they parted, Chloe told them about running from the police, how they wanted her because of her involvement in Piper's death. "Ruby said she would tell them to leave me alone, but she hasn't gotten around to it yet," she said with scorn.

Shada nodded. Sikya asked why she'd risked coming to the city.

"I've got some bad news," Chloe said.

Shada sat back down, and Sikya sat in the chair opposite her sister. Sikya gestured for Chloe to sit as well, but Chloe shook her head, preferring to stand.

Chloe came right out and said it. "Richard's dead."

Sikya gasped. Shada blinked twice, and Chloe wondered if Hollis ever took control of her friend's body anymore.

"I liked him," Sikya said, her voice full of sadness. "He was always so nice. What happened?"

Chloe told the sisters about the plan to upload another mind into Richard, about running him through the process of retaking control, and about how he'd jumped off the building.

"I tried to jump off a building in the city," Shada admitted.

Sikya stared at her sister. "Because you couldn't control your body?"

"It seemed hopeless. This was before the serum, before I learned to keep Hollis from controlling my body for good without it."

"You don't take any serum?" Chloe asked. She had trouble wrapping her head around negating Fisher's attempts at control without her injections, even though Fisher seemed to be resigned to his fate. Hollis, from her understanding, posed a bigger challenge.

"I ran out a while ago," Shada said.

Chloe's respect for Shada grew.

"What did you tell Richard about gaining back control of his body?" Shada said.

Chloe gave Shada a brief overview of the steps she had learned from Shada.

Shada sat for a moment, deep in thought. The other two women waited for her to speak again. "I've been wondering how important it is for whoever receiving the upload to be hijacked into first. I think that's the key. We were both able to find the light before the permanent uploads; he was thrown into the deep end and asked to swim. To be honest, I'm surprised he was able to get enough control to jump off the building in the first place."

"I'm not," Sikya said.

Chloe and Shada looked at her.

"What?" she said. "He was a stubborn guy."

Chloe nodded in agreement. She spoke after a break in the conversation. "One thing I've been talking about with Alfie," Chloe said, directing her words to Shada. "Do you think it's possible to upload multiple minds into the same body?"

"All edited into one unedited? I've been wondering that too."

Sikya's face gave away her surprise.

"Yes, edited into unedited," Chloe said.

"Are you considering taking on another one?"

Chloe admitted the idea had crossed her mind after speaking to Richard's son. "My first thought was to force more edited minds into unedited bodies. But I don't want anyone else to die, so then I thought, what if I host them?"

The mind inside Chloe's head began to protest but found himself silenced.

Shada folded her hands on the table. "With the serum, it might be possible."

"You could do it, with the serum," Chloe told Shada.

Shada shook her head. "I don't want anything to do with WestCorp. Look how they've forced me to live! Nothing good can come from working with them again."

"Alfie suggested you take on Ruby's mind. With both Hollises inside your mind, you could take over the company."

Shada smiled at Chloe. "There's already one target on my back, why invite more?"

Chloe now took the seat at the kitchen table that had been

offered to her. She leaned forward, both hands on the edge of the table. "The target was placed there by Ruby!"

"And Piper," Sikya added.

"Whom I took care of," Chloe said. "Since that one was my fault. But this would rid you of the Ruby problem!"

Shada admitted Chloe was right. "But I would never make it onto the island."

"Let me worry about that," Chloe said. She told Shada about the group meeting she'd been brought to by Richard and Tony. "I'm sure they'd help."

"There are a lot of variables to consider," Shada said. She wasn't convinced.

"Then, when you're in control, you can help teach unedited humans how to take control of edited minds instead of letting them come onto the island for the negative edits."

"Negative edits?" Sikya asked. "What do you mean?"

Chloe told the sisters about Ruby's plan to edit the unedited to be angry and impulsive. "She's offering them for free," she said.

"Why would she do that?" Sikya said.

"Her plan is to convince them the negative edits were designed and implemented by Michael Hollis," Chloe began.

"And then she'll tell them he currently resides in my head," Shada said.

"She's going to blame the whole thing on you? If I didn't know the two of you, I'd never believe the uploads were possible," Sikya said.

"It wouldn't be hard to convince them she's on their side. She could wait until a predetermined number of the negative edits were completed, then say she wasn't aware of the switch, throwing Alfie under the bus as well."

Chloe marveled at Shada's ability to grasp Ruby's malevolent intentions; she hadn't mentioned Ruby's desire to get rid of

Alfie and didn't realize this option was available herself. "How can you put the pieces together so well? She does want to get rid of Alfie . . ." Chloe said, her voice trailing off.

"I've spent a lot of time with a Hollis," Shada said, tapping her forehead. "One large maneuver to eliminate all of her enemies, seems like something they'd do," Shada said.

"It's disgusting," Sikya said. She leaned back in her chair and massaged her temples.

Chloe excused herself to go to the bathroom. On her way back, she stopped in the hallway when she heard the sisters speaking in hushed voices.

"She needs to be stopped."

"She's gone too far."

"What am I supposed to do? This is all you."

Chloe assumed they were talking about Ruby. She reentered the kitchen and sat back down.

"So will you help me?" Chloe asked Shada.

Shada's head tilted when she looked at her friend. "I don't know. How would we get Ruby to upload in the first place?"

Chloe thought for a moment. "We could tell her the upload was to reunite her and her husband, that it would be a quick hijack, but really it's permanent. Alfie would help—he'd have to help, if he wants to continue his work."

Sikya glowered at Chloe. "You think they'd just let her walk onto the island?"

"It would work if I'm in custody," Shada said. "I don't want to do it that way, but it would work."

Sikya's eyes opened wide. "Use you as bait? Are you insane?"

"There has to be a better way," Chloe said. "I just came up with that off the top of my head."

The three of them sat in silence, thinking. "What if she has to upload into you?" Chloe ventured.

Sikya urged her to elaborate.

"Well, if she was about to die, and the only way she could go on was to upload into another body, I doubt she would hesitate."

A thin smile crept onto Shada's face. "And I'd be there, waiting."

"All we'd have to do is get you onto the island. We could probably do it in the bunker."

Sikya crossed her arms. "I don't like it."

"Now, I'm not agreeing, but what then?" Shada said.

Chloe said Alfie would help with Shada's takeover of West-Corp, then they could begin teaching the unedited how to take over edited minds.

"I'm not sure that's a good idea," Shada said.

"Why not? The unedited could finally take over. It's what we deserve."

"If I'm in charge of WestCorp, the edits could be distributed evenly, to those who want it, without the need to take over the edited that already exist."

"You'd provide more edits?" Sikya asked.

"It's an option. Look, I'm not agreeing to anything, I'm just thinking through the possibilities."

"Well, if you decide to go through with the plan, we would know for certain if it's possible to upload multiple minds into the same person. Then I could do it myself."

Shada's eyes bored through Chloe as if she could see Fisher in the recesses of her friend's mind. "You're going to do it anyways," she said.

Chloe blushed. It was the first time she'd felt seen since she was a girl, and she wasn't sure she liked the feeling. "Nothing's planned," she said. "But if you don't capture Ruby, I will. And I'm going to need your help keeping everything under control."

Shada nodded; Sikya scoffed.

"So either way, you want her on that island," Sikya said.

"I guess so, yes."

"You refuse to leave her alone!" Sikya said before storming off. Chloe and Shada stared at the ceiling as they heard Sikya's footsteps come from above.

"She'll get over it," Shada said. "I'll let you know. Don't tell Alfie I'm considering it. I don't want him getting any more ideas."

Chloe promised she wouldn't, then got up to leave. "You might not need the serum, but I do," she said, informing her friend she was headed back to the island.

Shada smiled. "Don't bother trying to get on without it, you'll need it when you upload that second mind."

CHAPTER TWENTY-SEVEN

CHLOE WOKE up Monday morning dreading the start of another hectic week. Her day was spent escorting fresh-faced unedited from the city to the staging warehouse, feeling guilty the entire time. In order to get through the ordeal, she kept reminding herself that steps were being taken to upend West-Corp's scheme, that soon Ruby would pay for her deception. The one good part of the day was when Ruby told her the police investigation had been taken care of. "Better late than never!" she said with artificial cheer before retreating back into her office.

Chloe shook her head. After spending the afternoon waiting for Ruby to end their day, she headed to Alfie's office.

"Come in," Chloe heard after she knocked on the scientist's door.

Alfie asked Chloe to give him a few minutes to finish what he was working on, telling her that then he would be "all hers."

Chloe watched his facial expressions go through a range of emotions, from confusion to indifference, understanding to anger, as he worked. It occurred to her he might not be edited, or if he was, his edits weren't as numbing as the standard.

"I was just looking over the results of last week's edits," Alfie said.

"And?"

"About what you'd expect. They were all successful, and the newly edited have shown some worrying signs of impulse control. There's already been an attempted murder: one guy walked in on his wife sleeping with another man."

Chloe wondered if the couple he was talking about was the same one she had escorted to the warehouse on her first day a week ago.

Alfie turned to Chloe after a final click of his mouse. "What brings you in?" he asked.

"I talked to Shada," Chloe said. "She's said she wants time to think about taking on another mind."

"She'd better decide soon. She's our best candidate."

"She doesn't want anything to do with WestCorp. She's upset about going into hiding in the first place."

Alfie nodded. "You think she'll do it?"

"I think so. She's just being obstinate."

"OK, keep on her. We need her."

Chloe told Alfie the plan she and Shada had discussed. "Either way, we would need to get her to the island."

"You think you could handle uploading Ruby?" Alfie said. It seemed to be the first time he'd considered the possibility.

"If she doesn't do it, what choice do I have?"

"Wounding Ruby and not killing her will be difficult," Alfie said. The statement was more of a spoken thought, not intended to spark a debate or poke holes in the plan.

"There are people in the city who have that kind of training. They're itching for the chance to help."

Alfie raised an eyebrow, and Chloe told him about the group Richard had belonged to. "One guy, Tony, was with Richard all the time. He'll want revenge."

"You've been busy," Alfie said, impressed.

Chloe smiled.

Alfie leaned back in his chair and stared at the ceiling. Chloe wanted to ask him what he was thinking but trusted he would tell her when he was ready. After what seemed like forever but couldn't have been more than a few minutes, his gaze returned to Chloe. "If you're going to upload another mind into you, we should make sure it's possible by uploading a mind less . . . intelligent."

"Couldn't that make it more difficult to upload and control Ruby? She'd then be the third."

"That's what I couldn't decide. It seems to me there's a better chance at controlling her if you already know what it feels like to partition once. Keep them organized. Then, when she gets inside, you already know what to do."

Chloe wasn't sold but trusted Alfie's judgment. "Do you have someone in mind?"

"The head gatekeeper," Alfie shot back right away. "He's bred for size and strength, not his ability to think. Should be simple enough."

Butterflies erupted in Chloe's stomach. Those massive humans were imposing. She calmed herself down with the reminder that Fisher was more of a challenge than one of them would be.

"I would hope so," Fisher said in Chloe's head. "Everyone knows they're slow. Impossible to have a conversation with."

Fisher's confidence killed the butterflies once and for all.

"So don't expect me to talk to him," Fisher told Chloe.

"The two of you will be separate, don't worry." She looked at Alfie. "Fisher," she said as an explanation for her silence.

"Understood," Alfie said.

Chloe appreciated that he didn't ask the details of their back-and-forth.

"Having the gatekeeper would also give us a way to know the best way to get Shada and Richard's friend—Tony, was it?—onto the island."

Chloe confirmed his name was Tony.

"I should be able to take back control faster than with Fisher, right?" Chloe asked Alfie. She had a plan brewing.

"I don't see why not. Unless Fisher tries to take back control again, which is always a possibility."

Fisher told Chloe he had no intention of trying again. "I like experiencing the world. Last thing I'd want to do is give you a reason to banish me from the light."

"I ask because I want to take the poison before the next upload." She knew there was a chance Alfie would advise against it, but her bloodwork would give her away if she did it without consulting him.

Alfie thought about it for a moment. "You have the antidote, right?" he said.

"I do."

"I'll leave that decision up to you. I don't see a reason, but then again, if you can't take back control, you'd be lost inside your own body. I can understand why you'd take steps to make sure that doesn't happen."

Chloe would be taking the poison before the upload.

"When should we do this?" Chloe said. "Ruby's got me busy all week."

"It could be Saturday morning," Alfie suggested.

"These weekends fill up fast," Chloe lamented. "Yesterday I stayed inside all day just to recover."

"Do you have a better idea?" Alfie said.

"No, I was just complaining. It has to be then."

The confused look on Alfie's face reminded Chloe he wasn't used to dealing with someone who wasn't edited to be happy all the time.

"Assuming this works, we can make plans to capture Ruby. Whether it's in you or in Shada doesn't matter; we'd know it is possible to hold two minds inside."

"We'll need plenty of serum," Chloe said.

Alfie agreed. "There's plenty already made. We're good there."

"What happens when we capture Ruby? I know we said Shada would take over the company if she's the one to do it, but if she doesn't agree and I have to do it, what then?"

Alfie thought for a moment. "Not sure. I guess we'll have to sort that out when it happens. The people on the island could hold some sort of vote, I suppose."

"Whoever's in charge needs to fix the people who received negative edits," Chloe said.

"It shouldn't be a problem. They might lose the memory of their time spent since the edits, but I should be able to get them back to normal."

"Or perform the standard edits, if they want?"

"That's an option too."

"It would go a long way to rebuilding trust. Once this all gets exposed, the people of the city won't appreciate what we're doing here."

"I know. You're beginning to sound like a leader yourself."

Chloe ignored Alfie's probing compliment. "If others express interest in permanent uploads after finding out about me and Shada, we could match them up with edited volunteers," Chloe thought out loud. In reality, she wanted to force the edited into unedited hosts but didn't think a strong stance would be given space by Alfie.

"That was my initial plan," Alfie said. "Fisher had to be tricked because we needed to see if the process worked. Sorry," Alfie said. It was the first time he had addressed Fisher instead of Chloe.

Chloe sensed Fisher's indifference even though his mind never communicated the sentiment outright.

"What I'm curious about is how much access to the uploaded minds you'll have," Alfie said. "If we can perfect the process, and upload many more into you or someone else, could they form a sort of collective consciousness? What would their life span look like? Would they ever be able to exist without the serum?"

Chloe considered his questions. Part of her wanted to volunteer right then and there to receive more than just three minds, to upload as many as possible until she knew more than any other human in history. The internet held the world's data; a collective consciousness would hold both data and experiences. "I hadn't thought about that," she said, a small phrase that didn't betray her thoughts.

"Taking it to the logical conclusion: if there were multiple humans, each containing multiple minds, they could work together to control the future of WestCorp and the city. They could upload into another body when their body expired, giving long-term stability to civilization."

Chloe laughed. "You have too much faith in people."

Alfie asked what she meant.

"They would kill each other! Only one would be left standing. Whoever creates the collective consciousness first would have to be the only one."

CHAPTER TWENTY-EIGHT

At the end of the week, Chloe still wasn't one hundred percent sure she was ready to go through with the second upload. Some days she was determined to see it through, while others she worried about becoming lost inside her body. Fisher's continued protests to the introduction of a third mind into her body forced Chloe to double down on going through with the procedure, confidence inspired by his negativity. Her own doubt would creep in when she hadn't heard from him for a few hours. In a twist of irony, if he kept his opinion to himself, she wouldn't regain her determination, but each time he told her it was a bad idea, her resolve was strengthened.

One concern she had was that the two minds would team up against her. She wasn't sure how it would work, and even Fisher claimed he would never do such a thing, but she couldn't shake the notion. At these times, she was grateful for the serum and knew she had access to her body in a way the two edited minds would never understand.

Alfie informed the head gatekeeper, Valhall, that Ruby wanted to reward him for a job well done. It was common knowledge there had been no breaches in security, a fact

Chloe attributed more to the lack of threats than anything the oversized man had done or implemented. Other than the searches outside the train, there didn't seem to be any other security measures in place, and she was certain that with a little creativity she would be able to figure out a way for Tony and the rest of his group to get onto the island. When she thought about using a boat to get the group to the island, she considered the possibility that a more telling indicator of Valhall's success was the absence of boats off the island's shores, both private and commercial. She hadn't seen a single craft in the water her entire time on the island; maybe this was his triumph.

Chloe was sent to collect Valhall and bring the man to Alfie's lab early in the morning. She had wanted to stay out of the buildup, preferring to prepare herself for the additional mind's upload into her body. Alfie convinced her that by bringing the head of security herself, it would make the plan more believable, since everyone knew Chloe worked for Ruby.

Outside the nondescript building on the side of the island closest to the city, Chloe took a deep breath, opened the door, and walked into the barracks where the security guards lived. The dim lights showed a common area filled with chairs, sofas, and table games. Everything seemed to be stained or broken, signs of heavy use. There were three guards gathered around a television, their eyes glued to the screen and their backs to her. They were seated on normal-sized metal folding chairs. Each chair had at least one warped leg. In a corner of the room was a pile of discarded chairs, their legs bent past the point of being useful. Meal containers and remnants of old food were piled onto tables and stacked on the floor.

Chloe waited for the three men to notice her, but they provided no recognition. She cleared her throat and they continued to ignore her. Tired of beating around the bush and wanting to get the upload over with, she stood in front of the television, blocking the game they were watching from view.

"What are you doing?" the guard closest to her, on the right of the group, said. He leaned over to the right to try to see around her. "We're watching that!"

"I'm looking for Valhall," she said. It was her first time speaking the name, and it felt strange on her lips.

"I'm Valhall," the man in the middle said. "Now move out of the way!"

Chloe didn't budge. "We have to go," she said.

"Get her outta here, Val!" the third guard said.

"Fine, fine," Valhall said. He got up and stood behind his chair. Chloe stood still for a moment longer, grinned at both seated men, then walked back around them. She stood next to Valhall, behind his chair, while he continued to watch the game.

"Let's go," she said. When she spoke to him, she had to look up, since the top of her head didn't even reach his shoulder.

He looked down at her. "This is turning out to be more trouble than it's worth. I don't care about some useless award."

"Be quick about it and you'll be back here in no time." She felt like she was dealing with a child, not the head of security.

"Told you they're impossible to talk to," Fisher reminded Chloe. He was ignored.

Valhall tapped one of his friends on the shoulder and raised a hand to the other. "I'll be back," he said.

They both grunted.

Chloe hadn't considered the size of her target when she'd used her personal transport vehicle to get to the barracks. With a glance, she knew there was no way he would fit inside. She turned to Valhall. "Do you have a vehicle here? All I have is this thing," she said, pointing to her ride.

Valhall laughed. "I've sat on toilets bigger than that!" He pointed to a garage door. "In here," he said. He opened the door and walked into the dark room. Inside was a pair of oversized golf carts. The sides were exposed to the elements, and there wasn't a windshield.

The cart could've held two of the guards, or four normal-sized humans, so Chloe had plenty of room on each side of her when she sat down. She instructed him to drive them to the lab.

Alfie was waiting for them outside. He extended a hand and congratulated the head of security for a job well done. "Ruby considers you a valuable asset and regrets she couldn't make it today."

"Where is she?" the guard asked. His eyebrows crept closer together.

"She got called into the city at the last minute."

"I didn't see a flight plan," Valhall said.

Chloe could see then why he was in charge. She wondered if the constant suspicion had been edited into his DNA.

"It was within the last few minutes. Don't worry, everything's under control." Alfie extended an arm and guided the guard, who looked to be about one and a half Alfies in both height and width, into the lab.

Chloe followed behind the two men, trying to guess whether the guard ate one and a half times more food.

Alfie led them to his personal lab. Chloe noticed the machine used to upload sitting between two stainless steel tables and saw that the associated, modified helmets had been brought in. Valhall kept asking what they were doing there, that he'd prefer a nice meal over anything else, but Alfie insisted he would be pleased with the surprise and that he had to wait. "Not much longer now," he said. He asked Chloe to step outside.

Chloe's eyes searched Alfie's for a sign of what was about to happen. The scientist kept a blank expression. She walked out, shutting the door behind her, and pressed her ear against the door to hear inside. She heard nothing. Less than a minute later, at Alfie's instruction, she walked back in and saw the guard lying on one of the tables, next to the machine that would upload his consciousness. The helmet was already on his head, and his feet hung off the edge of the table.

"He doesn't need to be awake for this?"

"Everyone who uploads is sedated beforehand. This time, I just gave it to him earlier. Much larger dose than everyone else's though," Alfie said.

"How long do I have?" Chloe asked.

"I'd like to start within the next few minutes," Alfie replied.

Chloe retrieved the bag she had left at the lab from a cabinet under the counter. She withdrew a vial of poison, the antidote, and the picture of her grandfather. This upload felt larger than the previous, somehow more involved. When Fisher had been captured, she'd already known it was possible, since Shada had done it, but now the weight of her decision came bearing down on her, and if she wasn't so far into the process, she would have considered backing out. Looking at her grandfather, at the lines in his face, and remembering the time the picture was taken, she tried to conjure up the comfort the picture had brought her in the past. The feeling wouldn't reproduce; it hadn't after she had been hijacked, and since then she'd accepted a permanent upload. What the picture did do, however, was give her a lens with which to view what she was about to do, gave her hope about the future she was taking a small step to create.

After placing the antidote in her pocket, she unscrewed the vial of poison and drank it in one swig. It was bitter, but the taste didn't linger. She took note of the time: half past seven. She had until half past three in the afternoon before the effects would set in.

Chloe climbed onto the other stainless steel table and looked at Valhall. Next to him, she felt like a child. Her feet didn't come close to the end of the table, and her shoulders left plenty of space on each side, unlike the security guard, whose body took up the whole table. She put the helmet on her head and lay down.

Alfie rolled his chair between the two tables and punched the buttons on the machine. "Ready?" he said.

Chloe closed her eyes and brought her chin closer to her chest.

CHAPTER TWENTY-NINE

"Time to take back over," Chloe heard Fisher think. The darkness was all-encompassing, and his voice issued from all around her, as if she inhabited a sphere made of speakers.

She knew what she had to do.

Chloe found the faint sliver of light and allowed herself to see around it—since looking right at it would cause it to disappear—then drift towards it. As the circle grew, it took over her entire field of vision. Through the aperture, she saw the lab. She was seated on the edge of the table, and Alfie stood in front of her body, trying his best to calm Valhall, who had woken up in a different body without knowing he would be switched.

"What's going on?" she heard herself say. The words boomed from her mouth and were slurred, as if her tongue was too large. She attributed it to the lingering effects of anesthesia.

"Give me a minute and I'll tell you," Alfie said. He took out a penlight and shone it in each of her eyes.

The field of Chloe's vision shifted as the man in charge of her body turned to see his mind's previous lodgings lying on the adjacent table. Chloe found her breath; it was fast and shallow.

"That's my body!" Valhall, with Chloe's voice, said.

"I know, I'm figuring out what happened," Alfie said. He turned his back and consulted a chart lying on the counter.

Chloe assumed he was using his act to buy her time. This was why Alfie insisted that edited humans know what was about to happen. If the host wasn't able to take back control, a frantic mind could cause damage to themselves or those around them. Sedating the host's body wouldn't work, because that would affect the host's ability to take back over. She got to work decreasing the speed of her breaths.

Valhall began to calm down. Even though Chloe hadn't taken back control of her body, she had still been able to affect behavior. She wondered if Fisher ever did the same thing to her. Could he have calmed her down or stimulated her without her knowing?

"I haven't, but it's an interesting idea," Fisher said.

Chloe still wasn't used to the fact that none of her thoughts were ever private.

While in control of her breath, Chloe sensed Valhall was close to jumping off the table and breaking equipment in the room. This was a good sign; awareness of the body meant she was one stop closer to taking control.

"Put me back!" Valhall-in-Chloe demanded instead of taking action.

Alfie turned to face Chloe. "It's going to take some time for me to figure out what happened. I won't be able to put you back right away, so you'll have to wait."

"How long?" Valhall-in-Chloe snarled.

"Could be hours. No later than tonight," Alfie said. There was a hint of mischief in his eyes.

Chloe made her body take a deep breath. She felt her stomach expand, then her chest. She was pleased with her ability to sense her body once more, and it helped her lose the sense of disorientation the darkness had produced.

Alfie smiled. He seemed to know the large, exaggerated breath was a signal from Chloe.

"Let me give you something to help you relax." Alfie walked forward holding a syringe.

Valhall recoiled, not trusting Alfie at all. He twisted on the table so Chloe's legs dangled from the side, and he was about to push himself off when Chloe took total control of her body, freezing herself in place.

Alfie seized the opportunity and shoved the needle into her right arm.

There was still some serum in her veins from the morning dose, but the additional vial boosted the effects. Chloe felt her connection with the world around her increase. She could sense Alfie's heartbeat resonating through the inanimate pieces of scientific equipment in the private lab, creating within them purpose that wouldn't exist without his presence. She became aware of her own heartbeat and followed it to the end of the line, through her limbs to the furthest reaches of her extremities. It didn't take long before she knew she was back in control for good.

Chloe swung her legs back to their original position, looked at Alfie, and smiled. "What was my time?" she said.

Alfie looked down at his watch. "From when you woke up? Minutes."

Chloe jumped down from the table. When she did, her legs seized up and she fell, face-first, onto the floor. She was able to use her arms to slow her fall. She climbed back up to a seated position on the floor.

"Was it the sedative or was it Valhall?" Alfie said, concerned.

"Not sure," Chloe said. She climbed to standing and used the table for support. Out of nowhere, the hand she used to grip the table tried to rip the table over on its side, but she regained control before it could succeed. When Alfie rushed to her side, she kicked him in the shin. He doubled over for a moment before popping back to vertical, pulling air through his nose in deep, long breaths.

"That hurt," he said through gritted teeth.

"I don't know why it happened," Chloe said. "There wasn't a thought for me to block. It happened right away, like an instinct."

Alfie backed up and leaned against the counter. "They're bred, and trained, to respond to threats without thinking. To be fast. Looks like he might be faster than you."

Chloe placed both hands on the table and closed her eyes. Controlling Fisher had been a cakewalk compared to reining in Valhall. With Fisher, once she had taken back control the first time, he had more or less stopped trying, except for the one time when he had reached out to Piper. Valhall, on the other hand, couldn't help but lash out. She knew she would have to stay present with her body, in a constant state of vigilance. She inhaled, feeling the air fill up her lungs. She knew her breath was the key. She should have learned her lesson after the Piper incident, but now she couldn't forget: control of her breath would keep control of her body.

She stayed still for dozens of breaths, making sure she was aware of her body so Valhall wouldn't have the chance to take over any of her limbs. She wasn't sure she could maintain awareness of both her breath and her heartbeat at the same time, and leaving either one unaccounted for could allow for one of the minds inside her to take over. It seemed Valhall posed the greatest threat, so she ignored her heartbeat, which meant there was more space for Fisher.

She reached out to Fisher. "Do you sense him at all?" she asked the edited mind inside her head.

"No words, just anger and impulse. Best of luck," he said, chuckling.

Chloe looked at Alfie. "I need to leave the island," she said. "And get to Shada. She can help me."

Alfie nodded and didn't ask any questions. "Let me help you get what you need from your room," he said.

"No, I don't need anything else from my room. I just need to get to the city."

"What if he takes over again?"

"It's not so weird in the city," Chloe said with a laugh. "There's all sorts of characters walking around the subway. Some lady talking to herself, moving around with jerky motions, won't even be looked at twice." She thought for a moment. "Do you have some serum here? I'll need two doses."

"Staying the night?" Alfie asked as he retrieved two vials and a syringe. He handed them to her, and she placed them in one of the pockets of her backpack.

"Might be," Chloe said as she walked out the door.

Alfie walked a step behind Chloe through the lab, in case she lost control again and had the urge to strike out. He helped her into a transport then took a second, each of them riding alone. While on the trip, Chloe looked out at the bay around the island, surveying the horizon for boats. She felt relief when she didn't see any and somehow knew there was a system in place to deal with intruders if she had. She wasn't sure why these feelings and beliefs sprang up—she hadn't cared about the island's security before she knew Valhall would be uploading, but it was a gut feeling that couldn't be ignored. When she tried to ask Valhall about the security measures in place, she was met with silence.

Alfie kept his distance as he walked her through the atrium and to the tram platform below. Passing by the two guards posted at the bottom of the stairs induced a sense of pride in

Chloe, along with the confidence that everything would be taken care of in the event of an attack. She remembered Richard's gun, left with the guards when the unedited man had been brought to the island. While maintaining her awareness of every breath she took, she asked for it back.

"He forgot it when he left," she said as an explanation.

The two guards couldn't care less about who the property was given to, as long as it wasn't allowed past them onto the island. They handed it over before resuming their own conversation.

Chloe placed the gun into her bag right before her head jerked sideways. The two guards didn't notice, but if they had, Chloe would have pretended she was trying to crack her neck. She heard Valhall's voice inside her head for the first time. "This bitch has me trapped!" he screamed.

If she hadn't been forced to take back control of her neck, and therefore her head and face, she wasn't sure she could've stopped him from screaming with her own voice.

Chloe got on the tram and watched Alfie recede in the distance as it pulled away. She was certain the next time she saw him she would have full control of the mind inside her head, including access to his knowledge and memories. She tried to ask Valhall how the station would handle multiple intruders coming on the tram and got no response.

She felt the antidote in her pocket and knew she would have to wait until she could get past the silence before she considered herself safe from being lost inside her mind.

CHAPTER THIRTY

CHLOE WAS on edge around so many people. She couldn't explain the feeling, or why it was happening, but wave after wave of anxiety poured over her while she navigated the train system on her way to Shada. Since she'd never had issues with anxiety in the past, she attributed her heightened awareness to the presence of Valhall and his constant search for threats, although without him communicating with her in any way, she wasn't positive he was aware of his surroundings.

In the hub beneath the center of the city, Chloe took note of every exit and studied the train system's employees for signs of recognition. Every traveler who walked by was scrutinized. The presence of the implanted head of security didn't account for her awareness of police officers; she was wary of them herself, since the last time she'd seen any they were pursuing her.

The train departing the hub was crowded, with every seat filled and still more people left standing. When a fellow traveler sat down next to her, she worried her body would strike out. Instead, she seemed to collapse within herself, wary of the person's presence.

Chloe did her best to use the awareness of her breath to stay grounded, but she couldn't shake the confusion about how Valhall could affect her internal state to such a degree. Part of her wished she could go back to her uncaring attitude, her confidence that everything would turn out all right, but another part knew Valhall's constant searching was necessary. It meant there was something she could push back against, that she could take steps to negate him, instead of being lured into a false sense of security. She didn't want a repeat of what had happened when she'd first captured Fisher and he had surprised her by taking over and talking to Piper.

While she rode the train north, Chloe realized Fisher might be able to help her. Could he block out Valhall's manipulation of her senses by controlling her body himself? She knew how to block him. It would be a tenuous form of control, but better than nothing.

"I can try," Fisher said.

Chloe felt Fisher take control of her hand. In the past she would have blocked him, but this time she let him take it, knowing she could end the test at any time. Fisher moved Chloe's hand onto her thigh and tapped it twice.

"Now try to find my breath," Chloe told Fisher. Her chest rose as he took a massive inhale. When he allowed her body to exhale, the beginnings of a sense of calm lapped at the shores of Chloe's nerves, taking part of her anxiety with it.

"It's working," she said. She allowed the edited mind to take ten long, slow breaths. Fisher must have been aware of Chloe's plan to take back control of her breath, because he held the last inhale longer than normal. Chloe was about to force the exhale when the air was released.

"Just wanted to make sure you were still there," he said, laughing inside Chloe's head.

"Don't worry, I'm not going anywhere."

Chloe took stock of her situation. The man in the seat next

to her, short and wearing athletic gear, wasn't a threat. This realization caused her body to relax, and she took up more of her seat. The mass of people standing in the center of the aisles, holding on to either the pole running through the center of the car or the poles going from the tops of the seats to the ceiling, stirred up slight feelings of claustrophobia but none of the worry their presence had elicited before. There was still a strange pull to inspect and memorize the various exits, an awareness she appreciated because it made her feel prepared.

By the end of her train ride, she had relegated Valhall's ability to affect her body to third, behind Fisher's, with hers given priority. Fisher didn't like having to do anything.

"I was happy just seeing the light," he grumbled.

"Well, we won't be able to enjoy the world if we are always looking for threats," Chloe countered. "But it is necessary to have him searching for us. Just in case." She wasn't sure she'd ever referred to the combination of Fisher and her as "us," and she hoped she wouldn't regret placing trust in him.

"You won't," Fisher responded.

She responded, without direct words, by thinking about how Shada would be able to help her take control if she ever needed it.

"You have a lot of faith in your friend," Fisher responded. "I'll show you it's all right to have faith in me too. My body's most likely gone, and I'm not going anywhere. We might as well work together to get through the rest of your natural life in a state where we are both content."

"Maybe I'll let you take over and navigate the world while I rest," Chloe said. She liked the idea of Fisher using her body to perform the tasks she didn't want to do while she could turn off and exist in the background darkness. She knew why she hadn't thought of allowing Fisher to perform some of her less-desirable tasks before: she didn't trust him. But an ability to cede control to the uploaded mind could prove beneficial to both of them, another benefit to uploading she hadn't considered. Had Alfie foreseen this possibility when he performed the uploads? She wouldn't put it past him.

By the time Chloe got off the train at Shada's stop, she was confident in her ability to maintain an equilibrium with both Valhall and Fisher. She called the safe house, and Sikya was at the station within minutes to pick Chloe up. On the ride to the house, Chloe kept her backpack on her lap and felt the vial of antidote in her pocket, wondering if it was the right time to take the dose. She almost took it in the car, but she didn't want Sikya asking questions.

When they got to the house, Chloe found Shada seated at the kitchen table, staring out of the window with a mug in front of her, looking like a stereotype. Chloe laughed. "Deep thoughts?" she said.

"Always," Shada responded. She smiled.

Chloe slung the straps of her backpack over one of the chairs at the table then stood next to her friend. They gave each other one-armed hugs without Shada standing up.

"Any news?" Shada asked. Her eyes inspected Chloe's face.

Chloe shook her head. "Not from me," she lied. "I was going to ask you the same thing. Did you make up your mind about Ruby?"

"I'm not going to do it. But I'll go to the island with you and help you keep control. I have some thoughts on how you might be able to get it done."

"I'm all ears," Chloe said. She tried to sound nonchalant, but inside she was dying to hear what her friend might suggest.

"First, let's take some time doing some breath work." Shada got up and led Chloe into the living room. All of the furniture had been moved to the sides of the room, leaving the middle wide open. Shada sat cross-legged in the center.

When Chloe went to sit down, she found the tightness of her pants restricting. She pulled them up and tried to sit down again but was uncomfortable seated.

Shada watched her friend before offering a suggestion. "Sikya, can you grab some shorts from upstairs?" Shada called out to her sister.

Sikya ran upstairs and came back with the shorts. She handed them to Chloe and told the two of them she would leave them alone.

Chloe changed out of her pants, folding them and leaving them on the table.

Shada guided Chloe through a meditation session. Chloe wondered if her friend had been taught by someone, read books, or taught herself. Whatever the case, she found an increased awareness of her body when they were done. She thought being around Shada could be part of the effectiveness of the session, that somehow their bodies had resonated with each other, imparting Shada's control onto Chloe. Whatever the reason, she was also aware she needed to use the bathroom. She excused herself, left, and changed back into her pants when she got back.

"You were going to tell me your thoughts about uploading two minds?"

"Right," Shada said. She had been staring off into space, and Chloe's question pulled her back.

"You and Fisher get along, right?"

Chloe nodded. She had a good idea of where the question led.

"She's good," Fisher said, impressed, in a space Chloe alone could hear.

"And you know how to control him. So, when Ruby gets in there, just create a simple hierarchy. Allow Fisher to take more control than Ruby, with you always having the most."

Chloe pretended to consider Shada's advice. In reality, she was ecstatic she had come to the same conclusion on her own.

"As long as you have fifty-one percent, I don't see why you couldn't maintain the upload of multiple minds," Shada said. "In a way, it mirrors real life. As long as you keep fifty-one percent of reality, the rest of the world can have the other forty-nine and you won't lose your identity."

CHAPTER THIRTY-ONE

CHLOE WANTED to start the process of getting back to the island now that Shada had agreed to be part of the plan to capture Ruby. She was able to get a hold of Tensen through Sikya, who had his private number. When she asked him for Tony's phone number, the mayor hesitated for a moment before giving her the information. He asked her to repeat the numbers back to him, which she did before thanking him and hanging up. She called Tony and asked if he could meet her at the safe house that afternoon. "Could you bring everyone else too? We're going to need them."

Tony didn't ask any questions before agreeing. In fact, he'd seemed to be expecting the call. "We'll be there around two," he said, then hung up.

Chloe confirmed Shada was still all right with going to the island that afternoon. "We'll be escorted by Tony and his friends."

Shada told Chloe she didn't even have to ask. "It's not like I have anything else to do," she said.

Chloe and Shada spent the early afternoon trying to figure

out how to communicate with Valhall. Or at least get him to communicate with words instead of impulses and reactions. They needed to find out the best way to get Shada onto the island and, if they could, find out if there was any way Tony and his team could join them in infiltrating WestCorp. Their main concern was getting weapons onto the island, since Richard had been forced to forfeit his when he had gone with Chloe. Without the guns, there wouldn't be much use for the team to be there.

"Then why get them to come at all?" Sikya said. She looked over the top edge of her book. Most of the time she was silent, content to listen to her sister and friend try to untie the knot they found themselves entangled in, but when she heard something she had a question about, she didn't hesitate to ask.

"To make sure we get to the tram in one piece," Chloe explained.

Sikya furrowed her brow. "Tensen's mayor now," she said. "We can tell him to make sure the police don't bother us looking for you. They might even be able to provide an escort."

"It's not the police I'm worried about," Chloe said. She lowered her voice. "WestCorp has been performing a substantial number of edits over the past two weeks."

"Aren't people always getting edited on the island?" Sikya said, interrupting.

"She's not talking about the standard edits," Shada said to her sister.

Sikya's face turned from confusion to recognition then settled on slight embarrassment.

"We never know when Ruby's going to tell them Shada's responsible for their new . . . outlook on life," Chloe said. A gnawing feeling in her stomach made her stand up and rearrange her pants.

"They're going to be pissed," said Sikya. "Why would she tell them to come after her now?"

"Why does she do anything?" Chloe said. She sank down in her chair and put a hand to her stomach. It was in knots; she was overcome with worry. Could it be Valhall? The thought hit her like a ton of bricks.

"Ruby's already told them you're responsible," Chloe said, her tone neutral. It was as if she was tapped into a source of information outside herself, plugged into the universe around her, even though it was just the head of security locked away inside her mind. She wondered if this was how Shada felt.

Shada, who was seated next to Chloe on the floor, crawled over and sat down in front of her. "My name is Shada Gray," she said.

Chloe felt her head try to jerk to the side and knew Valhall was responsible. The look on Shada's face gave away her concern.

"Let them," she said, her hand reaching out and touching Chloe's leg.

Sikya, on her chair, let the book fall onto her chest.

Chloe let Valhall take over and instructed Fisher to pay attention in case he was needed to help take back control.

"Get her!" Valhall-in-Chloe yelled. He lunged out with Chloe's body and pinned Shada on the ground, fingers wrapped around her throat. When Sikya scrambled out of her chair to help, Shada told her sister to wait.

It didn't take long for Shada to reverse their positions. She ended up on top of Chloe, her hands pinning Chloe's shoulders down instead of wrapping around her neck.

Chloe saw her field of vision shift as her head swiveled left and right.

"It's nice to meet you," Shada said. She was calm, somehow calmer than before, a woman in complete control of herself.

172

"They're coming for you," Valhall-in-Chloe said.

"Who's coming for me?" Shada said.

"You know."

Shada smiled. "I want to hear you say it."

"The other city-dwellers who thought they were getting something for free." Valhall-in-Chloe laughed, a deep, booming laugh that didn't belong to her body and had never been issued from her mouth before.

Shada stayed still, deep in thought. Chloe was tempted to take back control but trusted her friend would let her know when the time was right.

"Do you know the best way to get someone onto the island?" Shada asked.

"If I did, why would I tell you?"

"If you don't, I'll have Chloe take back control right now," Shada said.

Chloe's new laugh reverberated off the walls of the rearranged living room. "There's only two ways onto the island: the tram or the helicopter. Unless you plan on taking Ruby's helicopter, picking up your people, and coming back without anyone finding out, looks like you're coming up from below."

"It's happened before," Sikya said.

Valhall snapped Chloe's head to look at Sikya. "You mean the one who killed himself? We knew he was coming and let him in."

Chloe was shocked.

"Alfie told us he was part of an experiment. He was to be allowed onto the island without his weapon." Valhall laughed. "You think we'd let someone on we didn't know was coming? The second they step on the platform beneath your precious city, we know all about the people who are on their way."

Valhall turned Chloe's head back to Shada, and Chloe watched her friend digest the information.

Shada's eyes narrowed, then closed. Chloe felt a slight awareness of her own heartbeat; then, as it grew stronger, she became aware of the resonation of its rhythm with her friend's. It wasn't long before Chloe was back in control.

Shada opened her eyes. Chloe blinked twice then smiled.

"It's me," Chloe said.

"That wasn't Fisher, was it?" Shada said.

"It was like you were possessed!" Sikya said.

Chloe realized she had never told Shada about Valhall, and that she had figured out Chloe had a third mind on her own. "No, it wasn't."

"Who is it?"

"Head of security. Alfie uploaded him this morning." Chloe sat up and wiped her eyes. "I haven't been able to read his thoughts."

Shada closed her eyes. She spoke with them closed, as if working through a problem. "It seems like he doesn't think before he speaks. Definition of shoot first, ask questions later. Without that lag, that censor of himself, there's nothing for you to read." Shada opened her eyes. "Try letting him control your throat. Your vocal cords. But keep control of your mouth. It might allow you to hear what he would say if given the opportunity."

Chloe did what Shada suggested and was amazed to find the stream of slurs he was trying to release. She looked at Shada, amazed.

"I think you'll have to ask the questions out loud, since he isn't used to an inner dialogue," Shada suggested.

"What do you want to know?" both Fisher and Sikya asked Chloe, one inside her mind and one sitting in the room with her.

The image of Richard's son approaching her in the street popped into her mind. "Do you want me to upload your friends in here with you, or should I leave them for someone else?" Chloe said.

Chloe heard Valhall threaten to rip the limbs from her body while she squeezed her mouth tight. She took back control of her throat, and the screams stopped. She didn't miss the glance shared between the sisters.

Sikya looked terrified, Shada resolute.

CHAPTER THIRTY-TWO

Tony arrived at half past two with three additional people. They were all dressed in black. A light mist was falling, and as soon as the team walked into the house, they brushed drops of water from their clothes. Chloe recognized the woman with the ponytail, but she couldn't remember if she had seen the two men. When Tony made the introductions, Chloe found out the woman's name was Cora and the two men were Gustavo and Tim. She had a feeling she wouldn't remember their names.

"Is everyone ready to go?" Tony said.

Shada had changed clothes before they arrived, taking off her comfortable loungewear, and was now wearing jeans and a T-shirt. She told the team she was ready.

Chloe said she needed a minute. She didn't need to change but still took her backpack with her into the bathroom. She laid out two vials of different sizes on the sink and stared at them. One held the serum Alfie had given her, and the other was the antidote. After spending time with Shada, she was convinced she had gained enough control over Valhall that she didn't have to worry about losing herself inside her body, and since seven of the eight hours before the poison took effect had already passed, she unscrewed the cap of the antidote and drank the blue liquid down in one swig. It was bitter and had more of a chemical taste than she remembered. She stared at the vial. Could the antidote go bad? It had worked the last time after having been untouched for so long, so she doubted it had a shelf life. If it was ineffective, it would have to have been a bad batch, which, unless both poison and antidote were bad, she knew wasn't the case. Maybe the seal was broken? She stared at the lid, looking for cracks and finding none.

Enough time passed that she began to doubt the taste was as different as she first thought. She attributed her second-guessing to paranoia.

The vial of serum, still sitting next to the sink, was larger than the antidote. She worried Valhall could still strike out at someone around her, making the serum necessary, but as long as she stayed in control of her breathing, she thought she could control his impulses. Plus, if she allowed him to communicate with her, in the way discovered by Shada, his impulses might not build up and erupt unannounced. Deciding it was more important to have Fisher around, she put the serum back in her bag.

When she threw her backpack back over her shoulders, the gun the guards had returned to her shifted inside her bag. She took off her backpack, withdrew the gun, and put the backpack back on.

"How can I get a gun onto the island?" she whispered, alone in the bathroom. A question for Valhall. She listened for his response.

"You can't," he replied. "The guards won't allow it."

"What if they are busy?" she asked.

"They won't be too busy to search you."

Chloe thought a distraction was necessary. Or maybe a sacrifice. The presence of Shada might be enough to keep their attention, letting her slip onto the island with the gun. If not, she would have to forfeit the weapon and come up with another way to force Ruby to upload, although she couldn't shake the thought that a mortal wound would provide the most incentive. Alfie might be able to help with that. It was something she could worry about later, once she was on the island and knew if she still had access to the weapon.

She walked back into the kitchen, where everyone else was gathered, holding the gun pointed to the ground.

"Where did you get that?" Tony said. His eyes were wide, as if he had seen a ghost. He must have recognized the weapon.

"The guards took it from Richard before they let him onto the island. I got it back when I left this morning," Chloe said.

"And what do you intend to do with it?" Tony asked.

"I need to get it onto the island."

Cora, the woman with the ponytail, rushed forward and held her hand out. Chloe handed over the gun. Cora checked to make sure the safety was on, told Chloe to turn around, and shoved the muzzle down the back of her pants after lifting her backpack out of the way.

"You'll have to hope they don't search you."

Chloe felt Shada's stare and lowered her eyes, embarrassed. She had a feeling her friend knew her plan.

"There's a way to get past the guards," Chloe said, hoping her confidence wasn't transparent. "I'll take care of it."

Cora looked at Tony, and Tony nodded.

"Will we be going with you to the island?" Tony asked.

Chloe considered telling the group of them to come as well. More people meant a larger distraction. She felt Valhall try to take over and let him try to speak but stayed in control of her mouth. She found out that a group of this size would be seen as intruders, and there would be reinforcements waiting when they got to the station below the atrium. If it was just her and Shada, there was a good chance they would encounter the two standard guards, but with more guards waiting for them, the chances of getting the gun onto the island fell.

"No, it'll just be me and Shada," Chloe told Tony. "We need your help to get onto the platform in case there are people in the hub who want to harm Shada."

Tony agreed. "Is everyone ready to go?" he said to the group.

Everyone, including Sikya, said they were. Sikya had packed a large duffel bag, and it sat on the ground next to her.

Shada told her sister she wouldn't be able to come to the island. "I know," Sikya said. "But I don't want to be in this house alone while you're gone. This is everything we brought," she said, gesturing towards the bag.

"Where are you going to go?" Shada asked.

Sikya admitted she wasn't sure, then suggested she go back to their old apartment.

"Why not stay at my old place? Nobody would think to look for you there," Chloe suggested.

Sikya looked at her sister. Shada shrugged. "Can you think of any reason why that wouldn't work?" Shada asked Tony.

"Not from my perspective. It's probably a good idea to switch locations anyways." He looked at Chloe. "Where's your place?" he said.

"Half an hour from here. Takes forever on the train since it has to go through the center of the city first, but with you driving it'll be quick."

Tony reviewed the plan. He said they were going to take two cars to Chloe's apartment. The first car would stay with Sikya at Chloe's, while Tony and one of the men would escort Shada and Chloe all the way to the platform below the hub. "Sound good?" he said when he finished.

Everyone agreed.

Two black SUVs left through the front gate of the safe house at a quarter to three. Chloe and Shada sat in the back of one, with one forgettable man driving and Tony riding shotgun. Sikya rode in the other, with Cora and the second man, either Gustavo or Tim.

CHAPTER THIRTY-THREE

Chloe watched her old neighborhood pass from inside the SUV. The weather contributed to the gloom, clouds overhead tinting everything gray. It was the ignored part of the city most well-respected citizens avoided at all costs, but it was her home. She missed the place, even the uncertainty of her walks home, when she crossed paths with all types of people and had to figure out what threats they might pose. There was a sense of pride at having made it out of her previous conditions and an understanding she would never have to live that way again.

This was all sterilized from inside the vehicle, behind two men charged with her and Shada's safety. For a moment she considered getting out and walking, to taste danger once again, but knew it couldn't happen.

In the alleys were homeless people inspecting piles of trash that materialized every night, their eyes bloodshot and faces gaunt from both lack of sleep and indulgence in various substances. There were rats walking on the sidewalk without a care in the world, staying far enough from people they couldn't be kicked but never running away to the dark. The groups of people who sat in front of abandoned buildings watched the two black SUVs pass, curious for a moment before returning to their conversations.

The two-car convoy came to a stop outside of Chloe's building. Tony told Chloe to accompany Sikya to the apartment, to let her in and make sure she was settled, before coming back out and continuing to the train station. "We'll drive around the block," he said to both her and the driver, not wanting to stay in one place with Shada in the vehicle.

Chloe thought it was a useless precaution, since the windows were tinted and nobody could see who was in the back seat, but she nodded and got out of the car before it rolled away. Sikya, Cora, and either Gustavo or Tim exited their vehicle and met Chloe on the sidewalk.

"Let's go in first," Cora told Chloe. She turned back to Sikya and her comrade. "You two follow."

Chloe led the group up to her apartment. The door was locked. A moment of panic set in when she realized her keys were still in her backpack in the SUV, which was circling the block, but she kept a spare on top of the light fixture opposite her door. She retrieved it and gave the key to Sikya after she unlocked the door. "This is the only spare, so don't lose it," Chloe said.

Sikya nodded, her face serious. "I won't."

The apartment had been ransacked.

"Wait here," Cora told Chloe and Sikya. She told Tim, using his name, to watch her back, and together they entered the studio apartment, searching for threats. It took less than a minute for them to designate the apartment as safe. "Come in," Tim said with a nod of his head.

The first thing Chloe noticed was the various stages of death of her plants. Some were brown and withered to near-nothingness, some drooped and looked like with a little water they could be revived, and some seemed not to have noticed her absence at all. Her ivy had reached out for the window, towards the sun, and had somehow been able to extend a stem across a span the length of an arm. Its tips rested on a book Chloe kept on her windowsill. She was thankful whoever went through the room—she guessed it was the police—hadn't bothered to dig up the plants, because nothing was hidden in them.

The dresser drawers were all pulled out, and the clothes Chloe had left behind were tossed on the floor. Her mattress was twisted on the box spring, its sheets left in a pile in the middle. She peeked inside her bathroom. The mirror had been left ajar and the drawers beneath her sink were emptied, leaving extra toiletries and cleaning supplies on the floor.

Sikya touched Chloe's arm. "You need to go. I'll take care of this," she said.

As much as Chloe wanted to clean up the mess and leave a comfortable place for Sikya, she knew her friend was right. The car couldn't circle the block forever. Chloe tried to apologize. "It wasn't like this when I left," she explained.

"I'm sure it wasn't."

"We'll make sure she's settled before we leave," Cora said. Tim nodded.

"Take care of the plants," Chloe said. "You might be able to save this one." She began walking towards one of the plants that still had a faint green hue, but Sikya stopped her by standing in front of her. "Go," Sikya said. "I'll save it."

Chloe thanked Sikya and left. While she waited for Tony's SUV to circle back around, a man on the far side of the sidewalk called out to her. "Hey!" he yelled.

She ignored him.

"Hey, you! You out here all alone?" the man said. He had on a stained coat, and even from across the street Chloe could tell it had been a long time since he'd seen a shower. The man stepped into the street, making a beeline for Chloe. He looked both ways and so did Chloe. He watched the black SUV turn the corner and timed his approach to coincide with the moment the SUV passed by her. When the SUV stopped and Chloe climbed in, she looked through the tinted windows and saw a mixture of confusion and surprise on his face. She laughed.

"Do you know him?" Shada asked.

"Sure don't," Chloe said. She leaned back in her seat, and the SUV pulled away.

Being home must have lured Chloe into a false sense of confidence, a space where her defenses were down, because Valhall took over and began to speak. The words rushed out before Chloe could stop them. "Chloe's going to force all the edited into unedited bodies," Valhall said, using her voice. Chloe took back control right away, but the truth was out. She was furious with Fisher, who was supposed to stay present so Valhall couldn't take control, but she knew right away he had allowed Valhall to speak.

Shada stared at her friend. "That wasn't you, was it?" she said.

Chloe was taking long, slow breaths and didn't want to interrupt them to answer.

"You don't want to just take over Ruby. You want to take over all of them," Shada said, her voice low. Chloe couldn't tell if she was angry, because the words were said as more a statement of fact, a new development to be accounted for. "What makes you think other unedited can handle hosting an edited mind?" Shada said.

Shada leaned forward and told Gustavo to drive to the train station closest to Chloe's home. Gustavo looked at Tony. Tony turned back towards Shada. "There are too many threats," he said.

"Do it," Shada said.

Tony stared at Shada, then turned to Gustavo and nodded. Gustavo made a U-turn and drove in the direction of the station.

"What are you doing?" Chloe said. Her breath was now under control, and she made sure Valhall didn't have room for another outburst. She cursed Fisher once more. He didn't respond.

"We need to ride the train," Shada said.

Chloe waited for Shada to provide an explanation. It never came. "Why?" she said.

"You think the unedited are wonderful and you've demonized the edited. It's not so black and white."

"I'm not saying it is."

"Was the edited mind inside you lying about your plan?" Shada asked.

Chloe considered lying but knew her friend would be able to tell. "No," she said, hanging her head. "All the edited will be gone by the time I'm done. I made a promise to get rid of them."

"And that's why we're going to the train station. I want you to see the difference between the facilities controlled by unedited and those controlled by edited and tell me again they haven't done at least some things right."

"You're on their side," Chloe whispered, appalled.

"I'm on no one's side," Shada snapped. "I just know they aren't all bad. They've done good things as well."

"If you aren't on their side, why are you protecting them? Stop listening to Hollis and help me get rid of them," Chloe said. It was hard for her not to yell.

"We can't ignore the fact that the technology exists. It's not up to us to control it; people have to be given their own choice. It's about free will. You're trying to close Pandora's box after it's been opened."

Chloe was about to reply when Gustavo announced their arrival at the train station. He parked the SUV, and they all got out. Chloe had her backpack slung over her shoulders, and the other three carried nothing. Gustavo made sure the doors were locked and inspected the area where he had parked. His lips pinched together; he was forced to accept the vehicle might not be there when he returned or, if it was, odds were it would be vandalized.

Shada pointed to the tent community below the tracks. "These are the unedited. These are the people you want to elevate by eliminating an entire population of edited."

Chloe had seen many of them at regular intervals, had watched the kids grow taller as they aged. "They just need to be given a chance," she said.

"Not at the expense of others."

The four of them climbed the rusty stairs up to level of the train tracks, then paid to enter even though the turnstile was stuck open. Chloe's mind raced to come up with a response to Shada, to continue their debate, but when she looked at Shada's relaxed face, she couldn't imagine her friend thinking anything at all.

Chloe led the group to her usual spot on the platform and stood waiting for the train. "They made their fortune at our expense," Chloe said. She thought of Richard, then the memory of her grandfather the hijacks had stolen from her.

Shada looked at her friend. "An eye for an eye makes the whole world blind."

"What's that supposed to mean?"

"It means that your plan makes you the same as them, not better."

"They have to pay!" Chloe yelled. Right away, she descended back into her breath, kept it steady so there was no room for Valhall to reemerge. She was tired of arguing with her friend and resolved to keep her mouth shut.

"Look at the shadow from the pillar," Shada said. The sun

had, for a moment, peeked through the clouds. She must have been tired of arguing as well and found something in the physical world to focus on. "It makes a right angle with the tracks."

Chloe nodded.

"And points right at the clock."

She looked at the large analog clock, broken ever since she could remember, and saw the time: 3:41. She looked at her cell phone and saw the same time displayed. The synchronicity of the moment wasn't lost on her. She felt lucky to both be on the platform and notice the clock at the same time. It had to be fate, and she believed she was on the right path.

The shatter of glass on the tracks drew Chloe's attention. "What was that?" she asked.

Shada shrugged.

Chloe grew suspicious of her friend. For some reason, she thought that the shatter could have been the vial of serum in her backpack. She tore her backpack off her shoulder and found the serum right where it should have been. She looked at Tony and Gustavo, looking for some hint in their eyes they knew what had happened.

Neither of them looked at her.

The sun disappeared back behind the clouds, and the train pulled up, empty. They were the first stop on the trip into the heart of the city.

CHAPTER THIRTY-FOUR

THE TRAIN FILLED up with more passengers as it approached the hub in the center of the city. At first, a handful of people boarded. When they got on, they took seats far apart from one another, everyone leaving the seat next to them empty. The exceptions were Shada, Chloe, and their two male companions. The four of them sat in two rows of two seats, next to each other, with the two women closest to the window. Every stop added more passengers, groups of young men who chattered then giggled at their own crude jokes and elderly women who sat with their purses on their laps, patience evident in their posture. The seats filled up when they still had a few stops to go before their destination; more people would board than the number who disembarked, taking their place and forcing the leftovers to stand.

Tony and Shada sat in the row behind Chloe and Gustavo. Over the speaker, a voice announced that the next stop was the center of the city. Chloe felt Tony's face next to hers. He'd leaned forward to talk to Gustavo.

"Don't look, but have you seen the woman sitting at ten?" he said, referencing her position using the face of a clock.

Gustavo leaned his head closer to Tony but kept looking forward. "She's been staring," he said. "You think she recognizes Shada?"

Chloe leaned over Gustavo and into the center of the aisle, pretending to look out the window to the car in front of theirs. Through her peripherals she saw the woman the two guards referred to. Chloe's first thought was that the woman looked like a mother. The hair around her full face was frazzled and looked like it had been colored in the past. She was wearing tights and sneakers and had a large bag with her that looked like it came from a grocery store. Her eyes were locked on Shada.

"What harm could she do?" Fisher asked Chloe. Chloe ignored the edited mind inside her so she could remain in the moment and listen to Tony and Gustavo. She wondered why she hadn't noticed the woman herself and thought maybe Valhall had given up viewing the world through her eyes to search for threats.

Tony reminded Gustavo that, even untrained, she was still a threat. "Remember, she's still a two-hundred-pound primate. If she's been edited to be angry enough, she could make life very difficult."

"PCP," Gustavo said, referring to the drug.

"Exactly," replied Tony.

Gustavo asked about the plan.

"Well, if she doesn't do anything, we leave her alone."

"Maybe she thinks Shada's pretty," Chloe joked.

Neither man laughed.

"But if she makes a move, I want you to subdue her while I take the two of them to the platform," Tony said.

"And stay on the train if necessary?"

"We can't risk her getting off the train. If she's been edited, her anger might make her continue to attack, keeping you occupied off the train as well."

Gustavo paused.

"Don't even think about tranquilizing her," Tony said.

"I wasn't! I was thinking about choking her out."

"It won't happen fast enough. I can handle taking these two to the platform on my own."

Gustavo looked like he took Tony's assessment as a challenge but didn't press the issue. "But what if there are others?"

"That's an order," Tony said.

Gustavo nodded, all business.

The doors opened at the center of the city. There were lines of travelers waiting to board outside every door. About half the passengers on board the train began to get off. Chloe's group waited until they would be the last, then got up and rushed to get off. Tony made sure he was between the seated woman and Shada. As they passed the woman, she screamed.

"This is all your fault!" she said while rushing forward.

Gustavo, ahead of Tony and Shada, was prepared. He turned and grabbed the woman, one arm around her neck and the other hooked under her armpit. "I got her," he said.

Spittle collected at the corners of the enraged woman's mouth. "You think you can take advantage of us," she snarled. She thrashed against Gustavo's hold. "Let me go!" she yelled.

The other passengers did everything to ignore the unfolding scene. Some looked down, and others out the window. The few who couldn't ignore got up and moved to a different part of the car. Most of the people waiting outside the door Chloe was about to exit went left or right, to enter through others doors, while a handful of braver individuals squeezed past, as if the screaming woman and the man holding her were an obstacle they had to tolerate.

"Go, I got her," Gustavo said.

Tony ushered Chloe and Shada off the train. They turned around as the doors closed and watched the woman struggle.

Gustavo let her go once the train got moving. She threw herself against the glass and yelled at Shada, but her words couldn't be heard through the door. The last thing Chloe saw was Gustavo's stern face waiting for the woman's wrath to turn towards him.

"Let's keep moving," Tony said.

Chloe led the way, with Shada behind her and Tony bringing up the rear. They rushed through the station at a jog, fast enough to draw curious looks from everyone in the crowded hub.

Feelings of anxiety bubbled up in Chloe's stomach, like words that needed to be said, and she knew it was Valhall. Instead of allowing him to lash out, she let him take over the formation of words while keeping her mouth shut.

"Get out of here!" Valhall wanted to yell. Self-preservation overrode his hatred of Chloe.

Chloe didn't need to ask why. Everyone's attention, ill-intentioned or not, increased the chances of a threat.

Bypassing the escalator, she led them down the adjacent stairs, clearing two at a time. They passed another level before arriving at the private platform, breathing hard. They were alone. Nobody else was traveling to WestCorp on a random Saturday afternoon.

The screen lit up, telling them the train would arrive in eighteen minutes.

The three of them walked to the center of the platform. Chloe sat down on a concrete bench, which Shada used for support, while they both caught their breath. Tony was quick to recover. His focus was on the staircase leading to the platform.

Chloe knew, from the change in the time remaining until the tram arrived, that it took her two minutes for her breathing to return to normal. She realized her decision to communicate with Valhall, to release the built-up anxiety from his unsaid words, had saved her from dealing with him trying to take over while she didn't have complete control of her breath. She followed Tony's gaze and watched the staircase as well.

A pair of small feet appeared on the step just below the ceiling. Tiny sneakers, blue jeans. The feet went one step down, exposing the child up to their knees. Instead of continuing down the stairs, the child bent over; Chloe saw the messy dark brown ponytail of a young girl. The child's eyes got wide. "Mom!" the girl yelled. "Are these the ones you're looking for?"

Her feet disappeared.

When twelve minutes remained, the young girl and her mother stood at the bottom of the stairs. The mother yelled at Shada from behind Tony, who had stopped her from advancing onto the platform and now held the woman at gunpoint.

"All I wanted to do was provide for my daughter!" the woman yelled. Her child vacillated between sharing her mother's anger and being scared of the man with the gun in front of her.

The woman's screaming continued for five minutes, until the tram was seven minutes away. She hurled every obscenity she could think of at Shada, then at Tony for preventing her from attacking.

Chloe was grateful the gun kept her in place.

All of a sudden, the woman turned and ran back up the stairs. Her child struggled to keep up. Chloe could hear indistinct shouts from above. Tony listened, then turned back towards Shada and Chloe. "She's telling everyone up there that you're down here."

Chloe attempted some quick math, trying to determine how many people had received the negative edits and the likelihood of them being in the hub at the same time. She got lost in the numbers.

With just two minutes remaining, a group of five people, not counting the daughter, walked down the stairs. Their steady march struck more fear into Chloe than if they had run, and she felt her face flush red. Her stomach turned over, and she allowed Valhall space to communicate again. "Get out!" he wanted to yell.

There was nothing she could do but wait.

Tony swept his gun from left to right, taking steps back as he did so, threatening the group to stop their advance, but there were too many of them. Chloe took a look at the clock and saw the timer display just one minute remaining. She looked back at Tony and saw his chest rise with a deep inhale before he holstered his weapon. The mother was the first to run forward. Tony caught her with a straight arm and knocked her down. In the space it took for him to knock her down, another member of the group, a middle-aged man, rushed forward. Tony lunged out, grabbed the collar of his shirt, and yanked, pulling him to the ground as well.

Chloe had no doubt Tony could handle their attack, if they were all attacking him, but since they just needed to get past him, he was fighting a losing battle. The remaining three rushed forward, all with hate in their eyes, and Tony was able to grab one, leaving two free.

Shada and Chloe prepared to stand their ground. The tram was set to arrive at any moment, and they needed to somehow get on without their attackers. Chloe stood in front of Shada and prepared to fight the two young women who were barreling towards her.

They tried to run past Chloe, one on each side, their anger making Shada their sole focus. At the last moment she crouched, stuck out her arms, and held the two attackers by the waist.

"Let us go!" they demanded, striking her back with their fists.

"Get out of here," she yelled. They were Valhall's words.

Chloe screamed. Tears streamed down her face.

Out of nowhere the two attackers were pulled back. Gustavo had returned. They had been at the platform so long he must have been able to get off the train, turn around, catch another, and run down to the platform.

The tram pulled up, and Gustavo yelled for the two of them to get on while he held the attackers.

Chloe and Shada got onto the tram and watched as Tony and Gustavo fought to keep the five edited humans from getting onto the tram themselves. It was a strange sight, watching two experts struggle without having to worry about their own safety.

Their angry screams ceased as soon as the doors closed.

CHAPTER THIRTY-FIVE

CHLOE REACHED a hand up to her face and wiped away her tears. The liquid on her face smeared. She looked down at her hand and saw blood, bright red, on the back of her hand.

The poison she'd taken that morning was starting to kick in.

Chloe shook her head, confused. She'd taken the antidote. She thought back to her time in the bathroom, her inspection of the bottle. Was the antidote compromised? Had it gone bad with a broken seal? She hadn't noticed anything unusual. She cursed herself for not bringing a backup dose with her.

She felt faint and used one of the seats on the tram for support, leaving blood on the stainless steel.

Shada stared at her. "You should sit down," she said.

Chloe didn't need to be told twice. Her stomach roiled. She attributed it to Valhall but didn't want to hear what the island's head of security had to say. Fisher's voice crept into her mind. "We aren't going to make it, are we?"

She knew there wasn't much time left once blood began leaking from the eyes. She wasn't sure that, even if she did have another dose of the antidote, it would do any good. Chloe looked at Shada, at the two thin scars that descended from her eyes, and chuckled to herself when she realized that the two people in the world who had captured a mind inside themselves had experienced blood running down their cheeks. A strange coincidence even Alfie couldn't have predicted.

The knot in her stomach continued to tighten, and she wasn't sure if it was because of Valhall or due to her impending death. She allowed Valhall to talk, not bothering to control her mouth.

"Someone switched the antidote," Valhall-in-Chloe said, the voice deeper than normal.

Shada nodded, an admission. Chloe felt like the air was taken out of both her and the tram as they both sped beneath the city.

"You . . . why?" Chloe croaked. She felt light-headed and lay down on the floor of the tram after placing her backpack on a seat.

"You had to be stopped," Shada said. There wasn't a hint of second-guessing in her friend's voice, no regret at the permanence of her decision.

"Stopped? We were in this together!"

"You wanted to eliminate the edited. They're humans too. You seem to have forgotten that."

Chloe closed her eyes and felt the tram shift on the tracks side to side as it traveled.

"When?" Chloe said.

"You were in the bathroom and left your pants in the living room. I put the antidote in a small jar and replaced it with glass cleaner. At the time I thought it was the poison."

"But it was blue."

"I never knew what color the poison and antidote were. I thought you had too much confidence after the capture of your first mind and didn't want you to take it before uploading Ruby."

Chloe thought for a moment. "This was before you knew about the third mind," she said.

"Correct, and I didn't know you had poisoned yourself earlier. But once I found out you'd captured the guard, I guessed I was in possession of the antidote. I was going to give it back until I found out about your plan to make the edited pay."

"No! That's not fair. This was all for the unedited."

"The lengths you are willing to go . . . you don't even realize what you've become."

Chloe had no response. After a pause in their conversation she said, "Give it to me and we'll go back to the city."

"I don't have it," Shada said.

Chloe knew where the antidote was. She opened her eyes. "You threw it onto the tracks," she said.

Shada closed her eyes and nodded.

Chloe thought she should be more upset at her friend for allowing her to die. Instead, she felt a wave of relief wash over her. She remembered her grandfather's farm, being next to the old man as he picked an orange from the tree, and hoped the sense of comfort the memory used to bring would rush back once she drew her last breath.

Shada sat down and looked at her friend. Chloe felt more liquid leak from her eyes and knew her time was drawing to an end.

"You have to capture as many minds as possible," Chloe told Shada.

"It doesn't work like that," Shada said.

"Do this, for me. I'm not saying you have to eliminate the edited, but the more minds you can gather, the more you can help. Think about your sister, create the world for her."

Shada took a deep breath. Chloe wondered if Hollis needed to be subdued or if the breath was to control her own emotions. She hoped it was the latter.

"Alfie will help. He's the only one who knows it's even possible," Chloe said.

Shada looked like she wanted to argue but instead told Chloe she had no intention of working with the scientist. "You put too much faith in him."

"What other choice do you have? You're already headed to the island."

"I know," Shada said. It was the first time in a long time Chloe sensed uncertainty in her friend's voice.

Fisher couldn't believe Chloe still considered Shada a friend. "She's the one who let you die!" he yelled inside her head.

Chloe explained to Fisher that Shada was doing what she thought was best.

"And still you defend her," Fisher shot back.

Chloe blocked her mind off to the edited mind, choosing to spend her last moments in reality instead of in her head.

The tram pulled out from beneath the city and began its climb to the height of the tracks over the bay. Shada looked at the island in the distance. "They're going to be waiting for me," she said.

It occurred to Chloe that Valhall might be able to reverse the train. She had to say the question out loud in order to find out. "Is it possible to send the tram back to the city?" she said.

Valhall answered right away, without pausing to think. "Of course."

Shada looked confused for a moment before she realized her friend was communicating with the voice inside her head.

Chloe gathered her strength, turned over, and crawled to an interface next to the door. She managed to stand up and rested a hand against the wall for support. "Reverse it," she commanded.

She waited for Valhall to take control of her hand, but he didn't take the initiative.

"Shada's going there to attack Ruby. You're supposed to protect the island," Chloe said.

Appealing to Valhall's sense of duty did the trick. He pressed a series of buttons on the touch screen and the tram slowed, then stopped, midway between the island and the city. A few more commands, followed by a prompt for a code, were entered, and the tram began to go back the way it came.

Chloe collapsed. Shada kneeled down next to her.

"I'm sorry," Shada said.

"You did what you thought was right."

"There are people on the platform who want revenge," Shada said. She retrieved the gun from the back of Chloe's pants.

"Tony and Gustavo are there to help you," Chloe said.

Shada returned to Chloe's side but didn't say anything.

Chloe closed her eyes. The strength it took to keep them open was too much to bear. She took a deep breath before appealing to Shada one last time. "Think about what you could do with multiple edited minds uploaded into you. You don't want to eliminate the edited? Then don't. But don't squander your gift. Do what you were made to do and change the world."

Shada looked out at the city they were fast approaching. "The city was created because humans worked together," she said.

"Let them work inside your mind to create the future," Chloe croaked.

Shada wasn't listening. She was talking to herself while Chloe was talking to her. "Without direction," she said.

"You can provide it. Both sides just need someone to bridge the gap," Chloe said.

A change in the air let Chloe know these words had punctured Shada's soliloquy. She focused on her labored breaths. Blood continued to leak from her eyes, never allowing the spilt blood to dry. The last thing she heard was the gun being cocked, then a shot fired and the shattering of glass. Air rushed in as the tram raced towards the city.

"Goodbye, Chloe," Shada said.

Chloe sensed she was the sole person on the tram. But she wasn't alone. There was Fisher, and Valhall, existing in the background of her consciousness. And her grandfather's smiling face waiting ahead of her. She exhaled for the last time and felt the comfort she had missed wash over her.

The skeleton of a memory persists long after the associated feeling has passed, a barren structure the mind can no longer fill. When Chloe's life ended, she was able to realize her ultimate dream, to leave the city and return to life on a farm, by bringing her memory back to life.

The decay of her body began when she drew her last breath. The collection of atoms that constituted her flesh would fall away, leaving just bones behind, until those too returned to the earth.

Death intensifies decay, but it's memory's sole protection against time.

COULD YOU DO ME A FAVOR?

Please help other readers learn more about this book by leaving a rating and review!

Then head over to my website authormarcoshernandez.com and subscribe to my email list. You'll hear about upcoming releases and deals you don't want to miss!

ABOUT THE AUTHOR

Marcos Antonio Hernandez writes from the suburbs of Washington, D.C. An avid reader of both fiction and non-fiction, his favorite authors are Haruki Murakami and Philip K. Dick — in that order.

Marcos graduated from the University of Maryland, College Park with a degree in chemical engineering and a minor in physics. Since graduating, he has worked as a barista, a food scientist, and a CrossFit coach.

Alternative is Marcos's fifth novel.

authormarcoshernandez.com